STALKER

A DARK ROMANCE NOVEL

DEREK MASTERS

ALWAYS BOOKED PUBLISHING

Copyright © 2018 by Derek Masters

All rights reserved.

No part of this book may be reproduced in any form or by any electronic or mechanical means, including information storage and retrieval systems, without written permission from the author, except for the use of brief quotations in a book review.

For those who believe in love, even when it takes unlovable forms, this book is for you.

DEREK'S DARK DESIRES

Subscribe to my Dark Desires newsletter and get a FREE copy of Riot instantly! Riot is a full-length novel that is only available to subscribers!

Once you have your free book, you will have the advantage of knowing when I will be releasing my next title, when I'm having special deals, and you'll be the first to know the next time I have some cool stuff to give away (you can unsubscribe at any time).

newsletter.derekmasters.com

1
NICK

"A lot of people in your situation don't get a second chance at life. We don't want to see you back in here again. Are we clear on that?" the guard asked as he handed me a bag filled with the belongings I had when I arrived.

"Yes, sir," I replied, not intending to ever be back as long as I could help it.

I took the bag into a small bathroom, changed my clothes and handed my uniform to another guard, who tossed it into a huge basket to be laundered and made available to the next person who walked through those doors with a build similar to mine.

I was ushered outside the building and into a small gated area, where I joined several other men who appeared just as eager as I was. It was hard to believe that the day had finally arrived. It sure as hell didn't feel like I was ever going to make it.

The first thing I did was suck in as much of the crisp morning air as my lungs would allow me to take. Sure, I'd been outside nearly every day of my stint, but the atmosphere tasted better on that morning that it had tasted in a long time. I'm sure it had something to do with the fact that in just moments, I'd be walking out of those prison gates as a free man. The only thing separating me from my freedom was a guard checking each ID was last time to ensure that the only men leaving were the ones who were actually supposed to go.

If I had one regret at the moment, it was that I didn't think to pack any clothes in the event that I was released anytime other than summer, which was when I was sentenced and began my sentence.

I was a wearing a pair of jeans and a white, thin cotton t-shirt that provided zero resistance to the cold, wintery wind that was attempting to cut straight through my body. My muscles flexed involuntarily, making me feel like I was being chilled to the bone.

I'd made a name for myself in prison with my hard demeanor. I never caused any trouble, but that was because I never needed to. My size was enough to keep most people at bay and the ones who looked like they wanted to take a shot at me? I made it clear that it wouldn't be a very good idea.

Now my touch demeanor was about to deteriorate all because my body wanted to be an asshole. I tried to fight it off but I couldn't. I started shivering like a damn child, teeth clenched to keep them from chattering together.

The clothes on my back didn't even fit properly. My t-shirt strained against my skin and my jeans, which were relaxed fit when I entered, were far too tight. I attempted to shove my hands in my pockets to keep them warm, but it wasn't happening. I was able to get them in as far as the knuckles, but there was no room for my hands after that.

I watched in awe as the gates slowly rolled open. Freedom had finally arrived. Almost as if on cue, the former inmates, most of whom had been relatively quiet, began running their mouths at the guards as they walked by. I found it funny how they'd had nothing to say inside but were undoubtedly turning into tough guys. I heard every curse word and insult in their arsenal, but I wasn't going to take part in any of it. That wasn't me.

Focusing my eyes on the pavement, I quickly made my way out, distancing myself away from the idiots. I looked around and watched as they all made their way into the arms of people who cared for them. Wives, girlfriends, parents, relatives. With few exceptions, someone was waiting for them. It was a luxury that I didn't have. All I could do is walk away. Alone.

It was strange to be unnoticed, especially considering my size and stature. Standing at 6'4" and weighing close to 260 pounds, the majority of which was solid muscle. I've never been a small guy. In my life, I've always preferred to jobs that kept me outside doing hard, manual labor. Sitting behind a desk or pushing papers are things that would never work for me.

During my prison sentence, the only thing I had was time. Thinking all the time drove me crazy, so I chose to workout instead. If I had free time, I was working out. It helped me stay out of trouble. I already had a pretty solid form when I went to jail, but I came out cut and chiseled. I was easily in the best shape of my life.

When I got sent to prison, I thought I was going to be like all of those other prisoners when it was time to be released. I had people who loved and cared for me as well. At least, I thought I did. The people I always thought would be there for me, turned their backs on me when I was inside. I noticed it happening when letters weren't being returned, and phone calls weren't being answered. I tried to tell myself that people get busy, but after a while, it became obvious what was happening. They were still living their lives and had no time for a fuck up like me.

Since I didn't have anyone to pick me up in their

warm car, I was left to walk. I didn't know what my future had in store for me. All I knew was what I was doing that night. Everything else would be taken day by day.

I was confident of one thing and one thing only. After so many shitty prison trays, I needed to get a real meal in my stomach. If I had things my way, the next meal I ate would consist of a huge steak and a much-needed shot of Jack Daniels.

The only things I had to my name were the clothes on my back, a bag with a change of clothes that weren't going to fit me any better than what I was already wearing, and a bit of cash that was leftover from my prison account. I didn't buy much from commissary because I knew I'd need every penny I could get when I got out.

Everything else was going to be for me to figure out. While everyone I knew and cared about had forgotten all about me, I was fortunate to have one friend who didn't care what anyone else thought and stood by my side from the beginning. A true friend that was willing to give me a bed to sleep in and a job at the construction company he owned. All I had to do was get to him.

In a world where everything else seemed dark and bleak for me, I was grateful to have at least one person in life who refused to turn his back on me. I'd never had any real family. Having grown up in a series of foster homes which made it no secret that I was only there so they could collect a check, I never knew what it was like to have a real family connection.

The only time a foster family honestly gave a shit was on my 18th birthday, and that was only because they wouldn't be able to collect any more money from the government for taking care of me. They couldn't get me out the door fast enough.

I don't like to use it as an excuse because as a man, I realize I am responsible for my own actions, but I can't help but feel that my upbringing had a lot to do with the bad choices I've made in life. Those bad decisions were followed up by even worse choices. What could have been different? What if I had been raised by loving parents who could have raised me better. Would I have still ended up in prison? Maybe, but I think it would have been a lot less likely.

Instead, I followed a dark path that saw me spend my days working at whatever construction site would have me and my evenings sitting in bars, getting wasted and seeing what kind of trouble I could get myself into.

Unfortunately, trouble found me one night when I wasn't even looking for it. I'd had a bad day at work, and this asshole at the bar would not stop running his mouth. I ignored it as long as I could, but eventually, I couldn't take his constant tirade, and I snapped. The end result of me losing my temper was five years in the state pen.

All I wanted to do was shut the guy's mouth. I never intended to put him in a coma. It was just a fight at the bar. There was no malice on my part, but that didn't stop the state prosecutor's from charging me with attempted murder.

I was determined to fight the charge and clear my name until I found out I was looking at 40 years in prison if I were to lose. I couldn't afford a reasonable attorney and the public defender assigned to me didn't even try to hide the fact that if the case went to trial, I probably wouldn't come out on time.

Instead, I accepted a plea deal that allowed me to avoid going to trial and only put me behind bars for five years instead of four decades. Even if it wasn't intentional, I did commit the crime so I was willing to suck it up and do the time.

You always hear a lot of horror stories about prison, but it wasn't as bad for me as it is for some people. A lot of inmates who may have flexed their muscles at a smaller guy left me alone because I had size on my side. Still, I was smart enough to stick to myself and not go looking for trouble.

Now that I was a free man, I wanted to do things a bit differently. No longer was I interested in being rebellious. Instead, I wanted to focus on actually being a contributing member of society. There was just one problem. I had no fucking idea of how to do that. All I could do was focus on keeping my ass out of trouble.

The reality of it all was that I wasn't actually a bad guy. I wasn't even all that much of a troublemaker. I just had a low tolerance for bullshit, and when people started shit with me, I made sure that I was the one to finish it. I guess you could say that I never really played well with others.

All of that was behind me. I was leaving it all in the past. My buddy was going to let me crash at his place while I worked to save up a little money to find a place of my own. After that, there was nothing but potential for me.

2
NICK

I have no idea how many miles I'd been walking, but in the grand scheme of things, it didn't really matter. Although it was cold, I had gotten used to it, and the weather was little more than just a minor annoyance, at least until the sun went down.

Everything changed when the sun disappeared from the sky. The wind chill plummeted, and it began to snow, leading all of the roads and sidewalks to freeze. I was getting chilled to the bone, and there wasn't anything I could do about it.

Up ahead, I could see the lights of the city where I grew up and where my life changed when all the bullshit went down. When I was locked up, I told myself that I'd never return, yet there I was, walking right up to the only city I knew.

After walking for what felt like forever, I finally came to a bar. This wasn't just any bar, however. It was the bar. The one where everything happened. The last place I visited as a free man. The place I was a patron of the night everything went south.

I'd come full circle, and I wasn't sure whether or not I would be welcomed inside. I debated not going in at all, but I was freezing. I didn't have it in me to walk any further.

Opening the door slowly, I cautiously walked inside, being careful not to draw any unnecessary attention to myself. The first thing I noticed was the delicious smell coming from the kitchen. It hit my nose like a sucker punch and made my mouth start to water instantly. I was already hungry when I was released, and after all that walking, I felt famished.

The bar was packed, which was going to make being inconspicuous quite a challenge. I'd barely made it through the front door before what felt like every head in the place turned. It didn't take long before the whispering started and I noticed plenty of widening eyes. Of course, when I returned the look, they looked in the other direction.

As long as I lived in the area, it was something that I was going to have to get used to. I did seriously injure another man, and these people didn't give a shit whether or not I had done it intentionally. All they cared about was the fact that I did it.

It also didn't help that I was such a large man. I'd been big ever since birth and only grew into my body from there. If I had a dollar for every time someone told me I should be a pro wrestler or something similar, I'd be a rich man. There wasn't anything I could about the fact that people were intimidated by me. I'd learned to stay to myself in prison, and that's exactly what I was going to do at the bar. Besides, I wasn't looking to cause any trouble, especially on my first day out of prison.

Ensuring that I didn't make eye contact with any of the customers, I grabbed a stool at the corner of the bar, tucked away from everyone and everything. Placing my bag on the floor, I sat down and enjoyed the heat of the building. It was the first time I'd been off my feet since waking up in a cell that morning and my feet were happy to have a rest.

"What can I get ya?" the bartender asked, snapping me from my thoughts.

"Let me get a shot of Jack, a Budweiser, and a steak."

"No steaks here, man. We're a bar, not a restaurant. I can get you a burger or a sandwich."

"Fine, I'll take the biggest burger you have back there with everything on it," I replied, disappointed that I wasn't going to be getting that steak that I'd built up in my head.

"All right buddy, have it right out to you."

While I waited for my food, I turned towards the counter and trained my eyes on the dark wood and wondered what it would say if it could talk. I thought about what kind of stories that bar could tell before shivering at the thought that at least some of those stories would probably be about me.

It seemed like it took forever, but the minute the bartender sat my burger in front of me, I felt like I was a little kid in a candy store. It was huge, but that didn't stop me from devouring it within a couple of minutes. Even though I downed it, I still managed to savor each and every bite. It had been years since I'd had a real burger and the hard hockey pucks that they served in prison shouldn't even be allowed to be called burgers. I had my doubts that they were even made from real meat.

That burger was exactly what I needed and the shot of Jack that I chased it down with hit the spot. I really wanted to order some more shots and enjoy my first night of freedom, but I only had a little bit of money and knew I had to be smart with it. It needed to last me until I started getting paychecks on a regular basis.

I'm not sure how long I was sitting at the bar before a hard slap made contact with my upper back. It was unexpected, and it took everything I had not to jump off my seat, turn to the person who did, and knock them on their ass. Fortunately for him, I took a deep breath, composed myself, and turned to see who the hell it was.

Instead of a dickhead trying to pick a fight with me, my best friend Curtis was standing there, arms open wide and an enormous smile plastered across his face.

"Well would you look at this big mother fucker?" he asked jokingly. "You were big when you went in, and now you're a huge fucking ogre. Get your ass over here and give me a hug, you gigantic son of a bitch."

I jumped up off the stool and scooped him up into a bear hug."

"Fuck," he yelled as I lifted him into the air. "Put me down before you crush the life out of me."

"How the fuck have you been?" I asked as I lowered him to the ground and shook his hand.

"I can't complain brother. You doing any more drinking or do you want to get out of here?"

I downed what was left of my beer and sat it on the counter, along with enough money to cover the food, drinks, and a small tip. "I'm more than ready to get out of here."

"Is there anything you need?"

"The only things I need are a hot shower and a warm bed. I'm hoping you can help me with both of those things tonight," I said, grabbing my bag and tossing it over my shoulder.

"Brother, you're gonna love what I've got lined up for you then. Not only do I have the guest room all set up for you, but it's even got a private bathroom with a shower. There's just one favor I've gotta ask of you."

"Sure man, anything. Just name it."

"All right, well Kim doesn't have any problem with you staying with us for a while, but I may have left out the part about you being in prison, so we can't let her in on that little secret. As far as she knows, you've been living in California and are coming back to town for work and to start over. You cool with that story?"

"I'll cool with whatever you want. I just hope that nobody sees me around town and lets the cat out of the bag. Everyone seemed to know who I was the minute I walked through that door behind you."

"Yeah, well this bar doesn't count. It might as well be a world of its own. I highly doubt you'll have anything to worry about once we're away from here," he told me as we walked out the door and headed for his truck.

"Well, you are the boss. I'll just go along with whatever you say."

"As far as all this goes, I think less is more. The less we talk about it, the better it's going to be for both of us."

We rode in relative silence during the nearly 45-

minute drive to his house, pulling into the driveway just before 9:00pm. I'd never seen his place before since he'd bought it while I was inside, not long after getting engaged to his girlfriend.

I was impressed by how well he had done for himself. The house was very nice, and from what I could, he didn't have any neighbors for miles. I hadn't planned to be in such a private place, but I was actually grateful for it. If there weren't anyone around, it would be tough for me to get into any sort of trouble.

As I followed Curtis into the house, I couldn't get over how much it looked like something you'd see on the front of a Christmas card. He shared the home with Kim, his live-in girlfriend, who I had never met since they met while I was in jail. Curtis, on the other hand, has been a friend since I was just a little kid.

We first met when we were placed in the same foster home. We were only together for a couple of weeks before the cops raided the house for manufacturing drugs, but we became close in that time. Over the years in the foster care system, the two of us always seemed to cross paths, and we made a pact to stay in touch. We've been friends ever since.

Curtis even visited me in prison when I first got there, although his girlfriend had no clue about any of that. In her mind, I was nothing more than a hard-working man from California who was making his way to Minnesota for a job opportunity with my old friend.

The first thing I noticed upon walking through the door was that the house was full of thick, plush carpet that looked like it had never even been stepped on. I watched as Curtis removed his shoes and placed them next to the door, so I followed suit and took off my wet boots and socks. My feet were sore and achy from the cold and all the walking I'd done that day.

"Just come with me, and I'll show you your room. You can take a shower and get cleaned up before you meet my future wife if you'd like. Oh, and I stopped at the store a couple days ago and picked you up a few pairs of pants and some shirts. I had a feeling you'd be coming out with clothes that didn't fit you and just by looking at you, I can see that I was right."

"Shit, you didn't have to do that man. I've got a few bucks I could have used for that."

"Don't be ridiculous. Besides, I can always dock your first paycheck. That's the beauty of being the boss," he joked with a wink.

The room itself was relatively small but looked huge compared to the two-person cell I shared in prison. It might as well have been a presidential suite at an expensive hotel. It had a television, which was more than I could say for where I'd been.

"Curtis, I appreciate you letting me stay here. I promise I won't let you down and if you need anything, I consider myself indebted to you for this."

"I don't need your thanks, Nick. You and I might as well be brothers. You've got to remember that. Just keep yourself out of trouble so you can get your life back on track. Anyway, if you're not going to get in the shower, you can come on out and meet Kim. I'm pretty sure Alexa is here as well."

Alexa was a name that I'd never heard him mention before. "Alexa? Who is that?"

"Alexa is Kim's best friend. You can never repeat this, and if you ever do, I will deny saying it, but she is sexy as fuck."

Curtis led me towards the kitchen. The closer I got, the more I could hear women talking, complete with laughter that seemed to be bouncing off the walls. One of the voices was on the deeper side, but still very feminine while the other was soft, smooth, and comforting.

Compared to the sounds I was used to hearing inside the prison walls, the soft voice had a comfort that made me smile. I wasn't quite sure why. Once I stepped into the kitchen, I was able to put faces to the voices. The first woman was tall, thin, tan, and had brown hair hanging just past her shoulders. She was cute and had a good figure, but she wasn't curvy enough for my taste. The girls were so lost in their conversation that they didn't even notice we had walked in.

The brunette continued laughing, allowing me to see that she was the one with the deeper voice. My eyes shifted to the other woman, who had the most beautiful smile on her face as she listened to her friend telling whatever story she was telling. This woman was shorter, only about five-feet tall or so, and had a creamy, pale complexion. She had blonde hair with brown highlights that fell close to the middle of her back.

My eyes moved from her face to her body. Even though she had a smaller frame, her curves were terrific. Her purple sweater was snug to her ample breasts, and her tight jeans showed that she had some ass to work with.

Never in my life have I been a shy person, but this woman made me nervous for some reason. My stomach began to turn, and my chest started to become tight. It didn't help that it had been so long since I'd been in the company of a woman and the woman I was staring at may have been the most beautiful woman I'd ever laid eyes on. As a matter of fact, I don't think the word beautiful does her justice.

If I had ever dreamed of what the perfect woman would like it, she would be the image in my mind. Just seeing her had me instantly aroused and I had to try to focus on something else in order to avoid a potentially awkward situation.

Eventually, the women noticed us standing in the kitchen and broke away from their conversation, making their way towards us. The brunette led the way, holding her hand out towards me and smiling.

"Hello, you must be the Nick I've heard so much about," she said excitedly. "I'm Kim. It's a pleasure to finally meet you!"

I was so excited to learn that the brunette belonged to Curtis.

"Hello," I mumbled, unable to get anything else out as my throat had suddenly become dry.

I turned my attention to her friend, who had joined Kim at her side. This gorgeous woman's lips were parted ever so slightly, and I couldn't help but think about what they would feel like against mine. I also noticed her blue eyes, which I'd always had a weakness for.

It wasn't hard to notice that she was checking me out as well. I watched as her eyes traveled up my chest and to my face until we locked eyes. She knew she was busted and turned away embarrassed. She had a smile on her face, which looked great on her.

There was one thing I was sure of. I wanted her in the worst possible way. I didn't even know her, and I already knew that I had never come across a woman like her in the past and I doubted I ever would in the future. I'd never wanted anyone as much as I wanted her. I felt like I needed her.

It didn't matter to me what I had to do. Whatever it was going to take, that girl was going to belong to me. I knew that I was going to have one purpose in life moving forward. That purpose would be her.

3
ALEXA

I didn't understand what I was feeling. I'd never met the man standing in front of me, but there I was feeling like a schoolgirl standing on the playground when her crush walks up.

"What's your name?" the attractive man asked in a low, throaty growl. His voice was sexy as hell and made my knees weak. It was almost hypnotizing. As a matter of fact, it was so hypnotizing that I didn't even realize he was talking to me at first.

"Me? Oh, hi, I'm good, thanks." I'm good? What the hell was I doing? "I mean Alexa. My name's Alexa."

Yes, I was that smooth. I couldn't believe how stupid I had just sounded in front of that man. He asked me what my name was and I replied that I was doing good? What in the hell was my problem? All I could was look down at the floor, embarrassed that I'd just made a fool of myself.

I figured I'd probably just ruined that before it even got started. Surely, he must have thought I was an idiot. Eventually, I got the nerve to look back up at him and could feel my cheeks burning with a rosy glow that only blushing could create. When our eyes met again, it felt as though he was staring directly into my soul. His eyes were dark, and his face was rough, yet still very attractive at the same time.

His face was scruffy and looked as if he hadn't shaved in at least a week. That wasn't a problem as far as I was concerned because I've always liked a man with some facial hair. He was also big. Massive would be a word that would describe him well. He towered over me, which was another plus in my book. If there was a guy who could make me feel safe and secure in his arms, I had no doubt it would be Nick. He was more than a little intimidating though, and I'd never been around someone quite like that.

He had dark brown hair. It was thick and a little longer than I typically liked, but it seemed to work for him. It curled just over the top, giving him an unexpected dose of boyish cuteness, even though it was clear that he was all man. Before I knew what I was doing, I found my eyes scanning up and down his body again.

Get yourself together Alexa. He's already caught you checking him out once. You're acting like a horny bimbo, and the only thing you know about this man is his name.

I was trying to get a handle on what my problem was. I never acted like that around a man, especially after what I had been through. My last few relationships had ended badly, and the last thing I wanted to do was get involved in another one. Yet, there I was, drawn to this handsome stranger, which was entirely out of character for me. I had no idea what it was, but there was something about him. When my eyes returned to his face, he was still looking at me.

What the hell am I supposed to do now?

I was afraid of once again saying something stupid, so I held my breath so nothing could escape my lips. I don't think Nick knew quite what to make of me, so he curled his lip slightly before looking away.

What was that all about? Did he just smile at me? Was he grinning because I'm acting like an idiot? Nice, Alexa. Real nice.

I glanced over in Kim's direction in hopes that she would give me a little bit of backup and help me out of the situation I found myself in. Instead, she smiled a knowing smile in my direction. The wink that followed the smile told me that she could read my mind like a book. She knew that I knew I was making a fool of myself. She could also tell I was attracted to Nick. After all, she had seen some of the guys I've dated in the past.

Not only could she tell, but she also thought it was hilarious. She was fighting back laughter, complete with tears in her eyes. If it weren't for her being my best friend, I'd wonder why I hung out with her at all.

I couldn't believe how quickly my heart was beating. I could actually hear my pulse in my ears. It was ringing so loud that I didn't have a clue what Kim and Curtis had been saying to one another. Before I knew it, Nick and Curtis were exiting the room, leaving me relieved yet disappointed.

"What in the world was that?" Kim asked, still trying to prevent herself from breaking out in laughter.

"What was what?" I responded, hoping that I could play dumb and make it believable enough for her not to grill me. It didn't work.

"Don't even try to play that off. That was the opposite of smooth you know."

"I don't have a clue what you're talking about," I insisted as I grabbed my purse and coat. "The only thing I know about right now is the fact that those roads look like they're getting back out there so I should be heading home."

"Mm-hm, I'm sure."

"You stop that," I told her, my face blushing. "Are our plans for tomorrow still on?"

"As long as the plows get out here and do their thing on time. Do me a favor and call me when you get home, so I know you got there safe."

"I always do. Talk to you soon."

"Okay, bye you smooth stalker."

I made my way out into the cold winter night. The chill in the air bit through me instantly and I was surprised by how much the temperature had dropped since I arrived that afternoon. The snow was really coming down from the sky, and the visibility was easily less than a quarter mile. Everything around me was covered in white, and it was beautiful. I inhaled deeply, allowing the crisp, refreshing air to fill my lungs.

Everyone has always thought I was weird, but I love the cold. Most people will tell you that their favorite season is spring or summer, but that just isn't true for me. I love winter.

I was jealous that Kim and Curtis got to live out in the country. They had their own little spot away from anyone and anything, and it's always so peaceful at their house. It was a stark contrast to the small apartment that I lived in. I was living on an assistant manager salary at the convenience store that I worked at, so I didn't make nearly enough for a place like that. That would change one day.

My job might have sucked, but there was a reason for my being there. I started as a regular cashier, but because of my work ethic, I was on the fast track that almost nobody was ever placed on. Within a few years, I'd be a general manager with multiple stores under me. That would make all the grinding more than worth it.

I didn't just use needing to get home as an excuse to get out of an embarrassing situation. The weather was really getting bad, and I knew it was only going to get worse. As the night wore on, the snow was just going to pile up even more. I got into my SUV and backed carefully out of the driveway, my mind still thinking about the man I'd met just moments before.

From what Kim and Curtis had told me, it seemed like he was going to be hanging around for a while, which meant I was sure to see him again, especially when you consider how much time I spent at that house. At least, seeing him again was what I was hoping for.

There was just one thing I was worried about. I've always heard that you only get one chance to ever make a first impression. If that statement was indeed true, I might be in big trouble. The only thing I could hope for was to make my second impression so good that he'd completely forget about the first. I was sure that I wouldn't be able to do any worse.

It took me forever to drive home in the snow, which

gave me a lot of time to think, particularly about the way Nick's eyes pierced straight into me. For the first time in ages, a man was giving me butterflies in my stomach. I couldn't remember the last time any man made me feel that way.

One of the things that attracted me most to him was the fact that he was so big and strong. I was sure that if you were to look up the word manly in the dictionary, Nick's picture would be there. Just thinking about him started to make me wet. I squeezed my thighs together. I just needed to make it through the ride home. I could take care of myself once I got there.

4
NICK

The room I was staying in had a view of the front driveway. I parted the blinds just far enough to be able to look out without being noticed. I felt a lump in my throat as I watched her back out of the driveway and slowly make her way up the snow-covered street.

Be safe beautiful. I'll be seeing you soon.

For some reason, my mind started wondering what her home looked like. I wondered if it was something like Curtis lives in or does she live in something more like the prison I was accustomed to. I had no idea what she did for a living, so I had no idea how she lived.

I also wondered if she was heading home to an empty house where she would spend her evening alone, perhaps reading a book or catching up on some shows on Netflix.

Was it the other way around? Did she have someone to go home to?

I realized how stupid it was that I was even thinking that way. She was a knockout. There was no way in hell she didn't have someone waiting for her at home.

Alexa didn't have a ring on her finger. I know because I checked. Still, it would amaze me if she didn't at least have a boyfriend. Even if she did, she probably also had a long line of guys banging her door down for a chance to take her out in the event her boyfriend ever fucked things up.

If there was a list, I wanted to know how to get on it because I would love to throw my name into the hat. Of course, what kind of chance would a guy like me have with a girl like her? She wouldn't want someone like me. I'm not educated like the guys she undoubtedly dates. Besides, when she looked at me in the kitchen, she didn't have a desire in her eyes, did she?

That girl seemed like one of the good ones and was almost guaranteed to be out of my league. After all, what did I have going for me? I was an ex-con who literally just got out of prison that morning. Of course, she had no clue about that and just knowing that my past was hidden was enough to bring a smile to my face.

As far as I was concerned, there was no reason to ever tell her about my prison sentence. Curtis was even keeping it from Kin, so I know he'd be the last person to say anything about it. If Kim didn't need to know, why did Alexa?

I grabbed my stuff and made my way to the bathroom. The thought of taking a hot shower sounded like a dream, and I was about to take advantage of it as much as I could. It had been years since I was last able to take a shower without having to see a bunch of swinging dicks all around me.

As quickly as I could, I stripped out of my clothes and stretched until I couldn't stretch anymore. The amount of tension and soreness in my body was unreal, thanks mostly to all the walking I had to endure. The fact that it was freezing outside only served to make matters worse. I turned on the hot water and watched in awe as steam started to rise from the faucet.

Prison showers had only two settings. Hot was what you enjoyed for the first 30 seconds, but as soon as that ran out, it was like being in an Alaskan ice field. That water was cold, but it was what we had to wash off with.

Catching a quick glimpse of myself in the mirror made me cringe. I looked like shit. Guys didn't spend much time looking into the mirrors in prison, so it's easy to let yourself go. My hair as a mess, my eyes had huge bags under them, and my facial hair was disastrous. I looked like the mugshot of every psychopath that's ever been arrested.

Even through all that, I could not get Alexa out of my mind. Even though I knew I had little to no chance with her, she was still occupying my thoughts. I highly doubted that I'd be able to land someone like her, not because I'm unattractive, but only because she deserved someone much better than me. She deserved someone who could give her a future that I couldn't give her. As much as that realization sucked, at least I had a hot shower ahead of me.

The water was much hotter than any water I'd felt at the prison. It was close to scalding, but that was fine with me. It didn't take long for my body to adjust to the heat and before I knew it, the hot water was enjoyable.

I stuck my head directly under the stream and allowed the water to run over me. Over time, the hot water started to dwindle, so I made sure to wash my hair and body before it was all gone. I planned on leaving my days taking cold showers behind me at the prison.

No matter what I tried to focus on, my mind kept going back to her. I didn't even realize how bad it was until I reached down to grab my junk and realized that it was already rock hard. I figured I might as well rub one out, so I wrapped my hand around my shaft and started stroking the length of my cock. If there is one thing I've always been proud it, it's my size down there.

All I had to do was close my eyes, and it was no longer my giant hand wrapped around my dick. Instead, it had been replaced with her small hand, barely able to wrap around my girth. I imagined her rubbing her hands down my face to my chest, scratching at my skin with her nails, which were perfectly manicured.

I pictured looking into her piercing eyes while she licked her lips, reached down and grabbed a handful of my prick. I could almost feel the warmth of her hand wrapping around me.

"Nick, your cock is so big," she whispered into my ear, her voice trembling with passion and lust.

My breathing became labored as she slowly pulled on me, moaning as she did it. She wrapped one hand around the base of my cock and moved it all the way up to the tip. Alexa applied just enough pressure when she touched me. She began stroking me faster and faster, my cock throbbing with each movement.

"You want more than just my hand, don't you?" she whispered wants again. "I know you do because I want that inside of me."

I could feel my entire body tensing up and braced myself against the shower wall as she jacked off my dick as fast as she possibly could. I got off with a lot of force, and it was one of the more mind-blowing orgasms I'd had in quite some time.

Unfortunately, that's where the fairytale came to an end. When I opened my eyes, she was gone, and I was back to reality. No, there was no way in hell I was ever going to let her find out about my past. I was going to find a way to make that woman mine, even if it was the last thing I did. It wasn't just something I wanted. It was something I needed.

5
NICK

I slept better than I'd slept for a long time. When I woke up, there was nothing but silence surrounding me. There was no screaming from cell to cell. No prison guards were flipping on the lights at 5:00 in the morning for count. There was nothing but silence.

At first, the silence made me freak out a little bit, primarily since I was still groggy when I woke up. If you're in prison and you're greeted with silence, something is very, very wrong. Silence meant something terrible was about to happen.

For a little bit, I couldn't wrap my head around the silence. There should have been inmates banging on their bars and screaming at the officers. Finally, I snapped out of it and remembered that I was no longer part of the system. I was free and never had to worry about any of that again. Once my mind was clear, all of my thoughts turned to Alexa.

I could still hear the sound of her laugh echoing in my ears. I could still see her gorgeous eyes and perfect curves. I was astonished by the way she was able to seduce without even realizing what she was doing. One look was all it took.

My mind drifted to wondering what she was doing at that very moment, and I wondered when I might be able to see her again. I wanted her to be standing right in front of me, looking up at me with those eyes that could melt steel. Seeing her again wasn't a want. No, it had turned into a need. It had to happen soon. I didn't care how I did it, but I was going to make it happen. That would have to wait, at least momentarily. I was about to begin my first full day as a free man and my first day back to work.

Since I took my shower the night before, I rolled out of bed, got dressed, and made my way into the kitchen where Curtis was waiting for me with a full pot of coffee. I filled my giant thermos, packed a lunch with items I found in their fridge, and the two of us made our way to the construction site.

It felt like it had been an eternity since I'd been out on a job site and I was excited to get right back to the only thing I knew how to do: work as hard as I possibly could. I hadn't been able to do any hard labor in prison since the jobs I was assigned to were things like mopping floors and washing dishes. It was great to be outside working with my hands and putting my muscles to work.

For a little while, I wondered if we were going to be able to work that morning since it was still snowing just a bit when I got into the truck. Fortunately for me, the work we were doing was on the inside of a retail space, and that job was going to last for at least a month.

Best of all, a straight month of work meant a full month of guaranteed paychecks and not the measly pennies per hour that the prison paid for their jobs. If I saved all my money, I'd be able to get my own vehicle and be well on my way to having a place to call my own.

Curtis told me that most of the jobs he secures are outdoors so I had high hopes that the weather was going to cooperate so we could move on to those. If that wasn't possible, I at least hoped he would be able to line up more indoor jobs so the weather wouldn't be a factor in whether or not I could work.

"It was nice meeting your fiancé last night," I said to Curtis, just making casual conversation so I could get to the real point of what I wanted to talk about. "And that friend of hers, too, what was her name?"

"Her name is Alexa," he replied. "Kim told me she was happy to meet you as well. She said you seemed nice. Best of all, she didn't suspect a thing."

"That's a good thing. I promise you that I'll be on my best behavior and won't cause any problems for you. So what about this Alexa girl? Does she come by a lot? What do you know about her?"

Curtis rolled his eyes because he knew exactly where this was going.

"Alexa is basically Kim's best friend. Does she come by a lot? Yeah, my house might as well be her second home. They are attached at the hip most of the time. Anyway, I believe she's 26, and she's an assistant manager at Conoco. She's on some kind of program where she's going to be running her own area of stores eventually."

"That sounds interesting," I replied, not sure exactly what I was supposed to be saying. "Does she live close to you guys? Sounds like the two girls have known each other for quite a while."

"Damn Nick, you sure are asking a ton of questions about Alexa. If I didn't know better, I'd think you might have a thing for her."

Holy fuck, I was feeling embarrassed. I could actually feel my face beginning to blush. All I could do was look down at my shoes and hope the feeling would go away soon.

"You're a damn dog, do you know that? A damn dog!" Curtis joked. "Kim and Alexa have known each other since they were kids. While she would love to live out in the country like we do, she doesn't right now. She lives up closer to St. Paul because that's where she works. She has her own place, doesn't have any roommates, and doesn't have any pets," he listed as he started to smile.

I stood there waiting to see if he was going to say anything else but he just stared at me instead, grinning as big as his mouth would let him.

"What about a boyfriend, man? Does she have a boyfriend?"

"No, she's single, but it's not because she has to be. Look, man, I know she's one good looking woman. Trust me, I sneak a look here and there when she's over. I'd never do anything with her, but Jesus Christ, how could you not? The best thing about her, though, is the fact that she isn't just looks. She's extremely intelligent. Oh, and she's so funny. She constantly has Kim and I cracking up all the time. She would seriously make a good girl for someone."

"Someone? Meaning someone other than me?"

"Honestly, she would probably be the perfect girl for you. God knows she'd be exactly what you need to keep you out of trouble. The only thing is, she isn't the type to have a one night stand or just a quick fuck here and there. As long as you've been locked away, I'm sure a relationship would be the last thing on your mind. I'm sure you're just looking to get your dick wet as quickly as you possibly can."

Little do you know that I basically fucked her in your shower last night. She just doesn't know it.

"Basically what I'm saying is that she is not easy," he continued. "She's also a tough nut to crack. When it comes to people she doesn't know very well, she tends to close herself off. She's had plenty of pain and heartache over the years, but you'll never hear her discussing it because she never wants to bring others down. She doesn't let many people into her life, and that's especially true when it comes to men. When she comes over, you're more than welcome to join us and talk to her and even get to know her if you'd like. I just don't want you thinking her panties are going to drop for you anytime soon because she doesn't go for that."

Sitting in my room after work, I started thinking about what Curtis has told me about Alexa. There was one thing he was right about. I had been locked up for a long time and may have been hornier than I'd ever been before in my life.

I didn't let the fact that I wouldn't be getting her into bed deter me from pursuing her. The fact that she didn't hop from bed to bed made her seem like even more of a challenge. It made me want her even more than I already did. These days, it's hard to find a woman who doesn't open her legs to half the people in the neighborhood, so the fact that she wasn't a slut was very sexy to me.

The thing was, I didn't want to just sleep with her. I wanted to get to know her on a personal level. Even more, I wanted her to get to know me. I know I can be intimidating, so I wanted her to say that I wasn't a bad guy at all. In the end, I hoped that I could have something real with her.

Even though I was all about Alexa, I was also a man who had gone years without feeling the touch of a woman. I needed to feel that touch. I needed more than that. I needed to get laid, and I needed it to happen soon.

It wasn't like Alexa, and I were an item. This woman didn't even have a clue that I was interested in her, so it wasn't like me going out and having a little bit of fun was going to be a bad thing. Even if we were to get involved, it isn't like she'd ever find out about a random fling I had before we ever got together.

"Curtis, where the hell would I go if I wanted to have to have a little bit of fun?" I asked after calling him into my room.

"That depends on what you mean by a good time. You

know what? Don't even answer that. I know what you're talking about. You don't know about these places?"

"No man, never needed to know about them."

"And why would you think I would know? You think I've needed them? Actually, don't answer that one either. There's a little club right on the outskirts of St. Paul. It's very out of the way, and you'd never find it unless you were looking for it. They've got some strippers in there who will pretty much do anything you want if you've got enough cash on you."

"Enough cash? How much cash is enough cash in a place like that?"

Curtis just rolled his eyes and reached for his wallet. "Here, I'm going to give you a little gift. Go out and have yourself a night of fun, but don't ever mention this to Kim. If she finds out about this, I might have to go there as well if I ever want to have sex again."

He gave me a hundred bucks, and I quickly shoved it into my pocket before going out to the dining room to have dinner with Curtis and Kim. It was pretty strange thinking about going to a strip club to find someone to screw. I'd never had to pay for sex before. I didn't really need to pay for sex then either because I could have found someone to fuck if I tried hard enough. I just wanted things to be effortless, so I could get off and get back to thinking about Alexa, not that I ever stopped thinking about her.

I made plenty of small talk during dinner, but I kept directing the conversation towards Kim's friend, and it didn't take her long to pick up on it. Through that conversation, I was able to pick up quite a bit of information about Alexa, specifically the name of the apartments she lived in.

Once dinner was over, I got cleaned up and made my way out the door. Curtis allowed me to borrow his truck for the evening, but not before letting me know that if I wrecked it, I'd be working for free for quite a long time.

On my way to the club, I stopped at a gas station to ask for directions. The thing was, I wasn't asking for directions to where I was going. Instead, I got directions to Alexa's apartment complex. From there, I drove over to where she lived and pulled into the parking lot a little after 10:30pm.

I actually passed the place a couple of times because they didn't look like the apartments that I was used to seeing. There weren't any big buildings. Instead, they were small bungalows that were side by side, each having their own individual yard and a couple of parking spots right outside the front door. The back of the parking lot was reserved for visitors, which is where I planned to park once I figured out which apartment was hers. Even though it was dark, it was easy to spot her vehicle.

I parked the truck in one of the empty visitor spots underneath a light that was either broken or burned out. I shut the engine off, killed the lights, and sat there staring at the outside of her apartment. I wondered what she was doing at that very moment.

There was only a single light turned on in the house. At that time of night, I could just assume the lone light was from her bedroom. She could have been reading a book or performing whatever nightly rituals she did before going to bed for the night. Right as that thought crossed my mind, the light was extinguished. It must have been bedtime.

Maybe she had to get up in the morning for an early shift at work. Curtis has told me that she was a manager. I had a feeling she was a great boss to the people who worked under her. She was probably very well liked.

It sucked being right outside her apartment, yet seeming so far away. All I wanted to do was see her. I leaned my head back against the headrest and closed my eyes. Immediately, I started imagining what the inside of her room may have looked like. I thought about how her bed must feel to lay in.

It was easy to picture her lying in bed, snuggled up under warm blankets. I could almost see her long, beautiful hair lying across big, fluffy pillows. Using a slow and deliberate motion, she would move one of her hands under the blankets, using it to reach down between her legs and rub herself over the top of her silky panties. She wouldn't rub too hard. Just enough to give a slight sensation to her clit.

Her lips would part, but only a silent moan would be released. I could see it so clearly. It was almost as if I was watching the entire thing play out on a big screen television. She'd slide her hand into her panties, brushing over the small patch of hair that was trimmed as close as could be, before finally reaching her clit.

Instantly, her fingers would feel her wetness as she slid them just barely inside her tight, perfectly pink hole. She pushed them in just enough to make sure they were slick. Using both her index and middle fingers, she rubbed her clit in a deliberate up and down motion, her breathing getting heavier and her legs spreading apart even further.

She continued rubbing herself faster and faster as she brought herself closer to orgasm. As she got off, she yelled out Nick at the top of her lungs, imagining that it was me giving her all the pleasure she desired.

I opened my eyes and smiled at how vividly I was able to imagine that. It may have been a little too graphic because I found myself hard as a rock. I wanted it to be my hands inside her panties. I wanted to be the one responsible for making her come over and over. I wanted to feel her warmth and wetness. I needed to feel her.

As much as I needed her, I needed something even sooner. If I couldn't have her right away, I was going to have someone. I knew I had to be patient if I wanted to be with Alexa. I really understood that fact. Until I was able to make that happen, I was going to see what the strip club had available for me.

6
NICK

I pulled out of Alexa's parking lot, not turning on my lights until I was entirely out onto the street. The last thing I needed was for her to spot the familiar truck. Following the directions given to me by Curtis, I headed for the strip club. It was just about midnight when I pulled in.

The building wasn't anything like what I had been expecting. I didn't expect anything fancy, but this place looked like some kind of seedy, run-down shack. The more I thought about it, the more I realized that maybe it was exactly what I should have been expecting.

After showing my ID to the oversized meathead at the door, I made my way inside. Some low tables were pushed right against the stage. There were a few random men in the building, but they didn't seem very interested in the things that were going on around them.

The appearance of the performing act on the stage matched the appearance of the outside of the building. The brunette, who was shaking it to the sounds of "Talk Dirty to Me" by Poison looked like she was strung out and, much like the men around her, appeared to be uninterested. I prayed that there were more attractive women somewhere in the building.

Looking around, I was able to spot a cute redhead at the bar. She was more appealing that the woman on stage, but she still wasn't quite what I was looking for. I decided the best thing to do was just take a seat in the corner and see what appeared.

"Well aren't you just a big, sexy man?" a voice spoke from the darkness after I'd been sitting for about twenty minutes.

I began to turn to see where the voice was coming from, but she slid into the seat across from me before I could. The beauty was much more like what I was hoping to find when I walked through the door. She had blonde hair, gorgeous eyes, a smaller build, and subtle curves.

"You just watching or are you looking to have a little fun tonight?" she continued as she reached across the table and lightly touched my arm.

I cocked my head to the side and shot her the friendliest smile I could muster without her realizing that it was fake.

"I may be looking for some fun. It all depends on what's being offered to me."

She looked all around to make sure nobody was within earshot before leaning over the table and whispering into my ear.

"Sweetheart, I can offer you whatever it is you want. All you have to do is tell what you desire, and I'll make it happen for you."

The beautiful stripper slowly slid back down onto her chair and watched me as she awaited my answer.

"I'm pretty sure you know exactly what I want," I told her, not willing to play the back and forth games that I was sure so many of those girls were so good at.

"Yeah, it's pretty obvious. Follow me."

She stood up, grabbed my hand, and led me away from the stage area and towards a dark hallway in the back of the building. She was moving fast, and I had to move quickly to keep up.

I definitely was no stranger to sex, but I could feel my nerves attempting to get the better of me. It had literally been years since I'd felt the touch of a woman. Hell, it had been ages since I'd even seen a woman without her clothes on.

Even with all the butterflies trying to work around in

my stomach, I was anticipating things to come. My cock and balls were aching for release.

I was led into a private room that looked much nicer than the rest of the place. Inside the room was a bed, an oversized chair, and a table with a lamp on it. The room was very dark, the lamp providing the only light once she closed the door.

"I could tell you were a big guy when you were sitting at that table, but Jesus Christ! I wonder if your hardware matches the rest of you."

Even with what she was saying to me, I could tell that she was just doing her job and trying to make me feel special. She wasn't actually interested in me, and as soon as we were done, we'd go our separate ways, and she'd be looking for the next man willing to pay her. I knew she wasn't there because she wanted to be. For her, it was all about the cash and that was fine with me.

I took the $100 bill out of my pocket and placed it on the table before taking a seat in the chair. Getting a closer look at her, she wasn't as pretty as I had initially thought she was. In the room, she appeared to have aged a decade. I tried not to think about that. If I turned off the light, it wouldn't matter anyway.

She took one look at the cash on the table and smiled.

"A hundred bucks? For that kind of money, I'm gonna

make sure you're very well taken care of. What's your name, sweetheart?"

"My name is Nick."

"All right, Nick. It's nice to meet you. I'm Tabby, and I'm gonna show you one hell of a good time."

"No," I said sternly.

"No? What do you mean no?"

"Your name isn't Tabby. As long as you're in this room with me tonight, your name is Alexa. Do you understand?"

Surprisingly, she wasn't phased by my request at all. As a matter of fact, it seemed like maybe it was business as usual and she'd heard it a hundred times before. She just nodded as she walked between my legs, spread my knees apart, and knelt down between them.

"I'll be whoever you need me to be," she told me, and she ran her hands up and down my legs.

"Do you think we can kill the lights," I asked with urgency.

"Sure," she said, rolling her eyes as she stood up and made her way over to the end table. "You ready to go now?" she asked as she came back and retook her position between my legs.

"As ready as I'm gonna be," I responded.

In the dark, it didn't matter what she looked like.

Without being able to see her face, she looked exactly like Alexa to me.

She ran her hands up my legs until she got to my waist and started fumbling around with my belt buckle. Eventually, she was able to pull it off.

I grabbed her hands before she could do anything else and pulled her up onto my lap, where she straddled me. Bringing her close in, I rubbed my cheek against hers, nuzzling her just a bit. Alexa wasn't there but, as far as I was concerned, it was her cheek rubbing against mine.

Softly, she leaned in and kissed my neck, flicking it at with her tongue as she grabbed my shirt and started to pull it up. She broke her kiss just long enough to pull my shirt up over my head.

She ran her hands up and down my chest and over my arms, feeling my muscles. Her neck kisses soon started to move down my chest and to my stomach before she slipped off my lap to unzip my pants.

I raised my ass up off the chair while she peeled my pants and boxers, sliding them off me and onto the floor. My cock was hard, standing tall and thick, ready for anything she was going to send its way.

I just wanted to fuck, but this chick decided she wanted to tease me first. She kissed all around my legs and thighs, coming just short of the areas that mattered. It was driving me crazy. Alexa was a great tease, knowing precisely when and where she should be touching me.

"I want you, Alexa," I whispered into the girl's ear, urging her to give me what I wanted.

Finally, she had decided I'd been teased enough and gave me what I had been longing for. She reached down and took my dick in her hand, giving it a good squeeze. I groaned loudly, not expecting the sensation to be so intense.

When you go so long without anyone other than yourself touching you, the feeling is intense when it finally happens. Just the warmth of her hand was almost too much to take and made me wonder how long I'd be able to hold on when we got down to the real action. I could feel the pleasure building in my balls.

She stroked me for a minute or two before I felt a warm wetness around my cock. She had taken me into her mouth and was sucking on it. I couldn't believe how good it felt. I could feel my entire body start to tingle when she wrapped her lips tightly around me. Even though I'm well-endowed, she was swallowing me whole. She was definitely a pro.

That thought snapped me back to reality. This woman really was a pro. She was nothing but a whore using sex to get money. She felt good, but she wasn't Alexa. I was in a room with the equivalent of a hooker.

I shook my head back and forth a few times. If I was going to enjoy what was happening, she had to be Alexa. Yeah, that's who she was. My sweet, beautiful, sexy Alexa in her form-fitting sweater.

It was Alexa kneeling down in front of me like a goddess. I didn't come to her to pay her any money. She'd chosen me of her own free will. She'd chosen me to touch and suck.

I thought of nobody, but Alexa as the pressure began to build once more with her head bobbing up and down as she sucked me into her throat.

With a handful of hair, I grabbed her by the back of the head, making her go faster, bringing me right to the brink of an orgasm. I pulled the handful of hair tighter when I reached the point of no return.

I erupted into her mouth and showed no signs of stopping. I could feel myself pouring into her mouth as she sucked and gagged, trying to swallow all of it. As my jerking started to slow, so did her hand.

When there was no more sperm left in me, she traced her tongue around my head, making sure she got every last drop.

As soon as she was done, my fairy tale was over.

She was no longer Alexa. She was just a stripper who moonlighted as a whore. I sighed, feeling incredibly disappointed in myself.

I stood up as she flipped on the light and got myself dressed, not really having anything else to say to her. She grabbed the money off the table and took a seat on the bed, watching me through her narrowed eyes. I'm sure she was wondering what my deal was, but I wasn't about to get into it with anyone, especially her.

Once dressed, I walked out the door without even giving her a second look and made my way out of the building and back to the truck.

I drove back to Alexa's apartment building, parking in the same spot I'd been in earlier. I sat there for the next couple of hours. I felt like a horrible person. Alexa didn't even know I was interested in her yet I felt like I'd just cheated on her.

I made a vow to myself that my next time would be with her, no matter how long I might have to wait. I didn't want to be with anyone other than her. In my mind, other women couldn't match up to her. Yep, the next time, it would be Alexa sharing a bed with me.

7
ALEXA

Sometime overnight, the weight of the falling snow knocked power out to my entire apartment complex, causing me to oversleep. If that had been the worst thing to happen that day, it wouldn't have been so bad. Unfortunately, the electricity going out was just the beginning.

It was absolutely freezing outside. I didn't have a clue what the actual temperature was, but it didn't take a genius to realize that the wind chill was well below zero. If anything, it made me grateful that the heat in my apartment was supplied by gas and not electricity or I may have woken up as a partial popsicle.

Determined not to let the fact that I was running late ruin my day, I got dressed as fast as I could and hightailed it out to my SUV. As soon as I put the key in the ignition, I knew exactly how the day was going to go. The usual dings and buzzing that I usually heard weren't there that morning. Instead, there was silence.

When I turned the key, nothing happened. Nothing even attempted to happen. The car did not make one single sound. The frigid cold temperatures had managed to drain my battery completely, and there wasn't a soul in sight that I could ask for a jump.

You'd think that would be bad enough, but not for me. The bad news continued. When the snow plow came through to clear the parking lot, it left a giant mound of snow right behind my vehicle. That meant if that by some miracle, I was actually able to get my SUV started, I'd have to figure out how to get out of my parking spot.

One thing was becoming clear, and that was the fact that there was no possible way I was going to be able to make it into work. Fortunately, I never take off work so I had plenty of personal days I could use so I wouldn't be missing any money on my paycheck. Of course, that didn't stop my boss from being pissy and reminding me that calling in wouldn't look good as far as my fast track program went, but I knew that my record was solid and he'd be able to get along one day without me.

It wasn't like he was going to be down a cashier. It was one of my office days so I was going to spend it doing paperwork, which I could easily do from home.

With that call out of the way, I didn't have to worry

about my SUV for a little while. Sure, I'd need to get things figured out that day, but at least it gave me a little room to breathe.

One bad thing about keeping to myself is that I don't have many people I can turn to when I need help with something like vehicle problems. I keep to myself for a reason, though. People have repeatedly broken my trust over and over, so I protect myself by not trusting people very easily. That allows me not to get close to anyone, but it also means not being close enough to most people to be willing to ask them for assistance when it's needed. There were two people that I knew I could count on, however, and that was Kim and Curtis.

Even though she isn't blood, Kim is the closest thing I have to family. She certainly treats me a lot better than anyone in my real family ever did. I knew I could count on her anytime I needed her. In return, Kim and Curtis knew they could count on me as well. Once I got back into the house and warmed up for a minute, I called Kim.

"Holy shit, do you have nearly as much snow as we got?" she asked, not bothering to say hello first. "I think the weatherman undershot this by at least 12-inches."

"Yeah, I got nailed with it. Plus, it's cold as hell, which is why I hate that I'm calling you guys to see if I can ask a favor."

"That doesn't sound good. What's going on?"

"It's this stupid vehicle of mine. It won't start. The battery is completely drained, and everyone else has enough sense to stay inside, so there isn't anyone outside to ask for a jump. I was wondering if maybe you guys could give me a hand."

"Of course we will, but it's gonna be a little bit. Curtis has indoor jobs, and he's already long gone for the day. We can come by when after he gets home if that's not too late."

"No, that'll be perfect. I've already called into work so I'll be here all day. I'll even make dinner for you guys."

Not only did Curtis run his construction company, but he also knew just about everything there was to know about cars. As well as he does with his business, I bet he could make a killing as a mechanic, but he likes what he does. He does love hearing Kim and I telling him how good he is at working on the cars, though. He's a man, and he loves having that ego of his stroked.

I spent the day in my living room, doing all the administrative tasks I would have done in the tiny back office at work. I'm always telling my boss that he should just let me work at home on office days, but for some reason, he insists that I be there to do the work. I'm sure it was driving him nuts that I wasn't there.

Even though it was simple work, I was finding it difficult to complete. My mind kept drifting in another direction, which was never usually a problem because once I focus on something, it's hard to divert my attention. Today, my mind kept thinking about the enormous stranger who was staying in my best friend's guest room.

I'd never meet anyone like him and especially not someone who made me weak in the knees just by being in the same room. He was the perfect combination of ruggedness and attractiveness. I had no idea when it would happen, but I was already looking forward to running into him again.

Would I run into him next week? Would it happen next month? What if he tagged along with Kim and Curtis to help me with my vehicle? That would be awesome, and it was definitely what I was hoping for,

Even though I knew nothing about him, I had the unshakeable feeling that I needed to see him. I hoped he'd be wearing a form-fitting t-shirt that showed off his muscular body and left next to nothing to the imagination. His arms were so thick and perfect, and all I needed was to feel them wrapped around my body.

These thoughts were pretty alarming to me because I'm not typically someone who has sex on the mind all the time, but I could not prevent myself from wondering if the thickness of his body translated downstairs as well. After all, a man the size of Nick has to be packing some heat, right? I wanted to know what it looked like, what it felt like in my mouth, what it felt like inside of me.

It had been quite a long time since I'd been intimate with someone other than myself. That wasn't what I missed the most, though. What I really missed was having a man to wrap his strong arms around me and hold me while we both fell asleep. I couldn't even remember the last time I felt the electricity when someone's lips kissed mine or when a warm tongue came in contact with my clit.

Shaking my head, I snapped myself out of the fantasy I found myself in, I looked around the room, almost expecting someone to be standing there who knew what I was thinking. Even though the notion was ridiculous, I was still embarrassed enough to make myself blush. I couldn't believe I was fantasizing about a man I knew nothing about, but there was something there. I just knew it.

There had to be some reason I hadn't been able to get him out of my head lately. There was no way I could deny the instant attraction that I felt for him and wondered if he'd felt the same way about me.

Oh, what in the hell was I thinking? There was no way he was thinking anything of the sort about me. I know I'm far from ugly, but I've been cheated on by everyone I've ever been with.

I've been emotionally abused in one way or another by most of the men I've dated. It's been enough to give me a complex about myself. I always have a problem with not feeling pretty enough or feeling like I'm not good enough for people. Doubting myself is probably my biggest flaw.

Later that afternoon, I received a text message from Kim.

Hey, we're about to head your way. You still up for making dinner?

Yeah, I'll whip something up.

Yay! You have enough for an extra mouth? Nick was wondering if he could come with us.

Sure thing. Hope he likes pasta.

Holy shit! He was actually coming to my apartment. As soon as I read his name, I felt the butterflies developing in my stomach as I jumped up off my couch and ran into the background to check myself in the mirror.

I touched up my makeup and made sure my hair was looking presentable before he came over. I wanted to look as good as I possibly could when he got there, just in case.

Once I was made up enough for my liking, I needed to get out of my sweatpants and old t-shirt. I changed into a pair of jeans that I knew made my ass look fantastic and my favorite gray sweater. I knew they'd be a bit, so I got started on dinner. Knowing that Curtis and Nick had worked all day, I was sure they'd be starving.

I brought a pot of water to a boil and threw in some spaghetti before cutting up some crusty bread that I'd bought at an Italian bakery the day before. I wasn't a great cook by any means.

The pasta sauce was coming straight from a jar but I did spice it up with some garlic, and a bit of sugar, which I always joked was my secret recipe. After that, I made up a salad and sat out a few dressing options before setting the table for four.

The spaghetti was still cooking on the stove when I heard knocking on my door. I knew I didn't have to say anything. Kim and I always walked right into each other's homes and today was no exception.

"Hey girlie," Kim yelled out as she wiped her snowy shows on the mat in front of my door. "It's just me. I've already put the boys to work trying to get your car out from all that snow." She laughed as she took off her coat and joined me in the kitchen. "Your boyfriend is out there," she said with a smile, making some weird up and down thing with her eyebrows.

I didn't know what to say to her, so I just smiled and nodded back at her, acting like I was concentrating on the noodles that were basically cooking themselves.

She tried everything to get me to talk about him, but I was remaining silent on that subject. Finally, she changed the subject to how cold it was outside as I mixed the sauce with the noodles.

They must have had some kind of radar in their stomachs because as soon as the food was done, the men came in from outside. I watched Nick as he made his way inside my place, his eyes scanning his surroundings.

I wondered what he thought about my little apartment. Did he like it? Did he think it smelled good? Did it look clean? Suddenly, I was paranoid, wondering if I should have given my house a deep clean.

Eventually, his eyes made their way over to me, and I met him with a smile, this time looking him straight in the eye. I liked his eyes.

They were so big. He nodded at me and smiled back. He took off his sock cap, exposing his hair that was disheveled from wearing it. He didn't look nearly as imposing as he had before. He now resembled a giant teddy bear.

Nick broke my gaze and looked me up and down before bringing his eyes back to mine. Knowing he was checking me out excited me. Hopefully, he was happy with what he'd seen so far. After that, we just kind of looked at each other in silence.

I finally looked away, telling everyone that dinner was ready. I sat down and looked up at Nick, only to find him staring back at me. The butterflies made a comeback in my stomach, fluttering all around. Why was he still looking at me like that? Was there something wrong? What was going on in that mind of his?

"Have a seat big guy," I said with a giggle, trying to joke away the intense stare he was giving me. He almost looked like he was in a daze. Eventually, he blinked his eyes, smiled and took the seat directly across from me.

"Thank you very much," he mumbled, looking at the food as he licked his lips. He looked over the offerings at the table, his eyes looking as hungry as he probably was. "Looks like you can cook," he laughed, smiling at me the entire time.

"Well, I can cook some things really well, but I wouldn't get too excited. Culinary arts were never my specialty," I joked. "I wanna thank you guys for coming over to help me with my car. I know the weather sucks out there."

Curtis started to tell me that the problem with my SUV was that the battery was dead, as if I didn't already know that. Still, I let him explain it.

I've learned that's one thing guys love to do. As was typical of him, his tale about my car quickly turned into a conversation about their day at the job site and some funny stories about people they worked with.

I wasn't interested until Curtis started telling me

about he and Nick met when they were in foster care and gave me a bit of their history.

Once everyone was done eating, we sat at the table talking and joking with one another. I was feeling a lot more at ease, and I was actually starting to get to know Nick a little better.

Much to my surprise, Nick became much more talkative as we ate, asking me more and more about myself. I was excited that he seemed to be interested in me.

He may have just been being polite since he was at my house but he seemed like he genuinely wanted to know more about me.

I asked Nick some things about him as well, but he wasn't giving up information very easily. He didn't seem like he was all that interested in telling me anything about himself. We sat at the table until a little before 10.

"We hate to cut this short, but we've got to get home. Got a long day of work tomorrow," Curtis said.

"Oh okay, well thanks for coming you guys. I really appreciate your help."

"It's not a problem. Thanks for dinner."

"I owe you one," I said, making sure I was looking Nick in the eye while I said it. "If there's anything you ever need. You make sure to let me know," I smiled, letting him know I was being genuine.

I said that to him as a way to gauge his reaction, and

he didn't disappoint. The look on his face was one of excitement and gratefulness. I was sure he was wondering exactly what it was I meant by the comment. His expression brought the butterflies out in my stomach once again.

"I'll be sure to keep that in mind. I'm sure I'll take you up on that someday soon," he said, maintaining eye contact the entire time. He didn't stop looking at me even as he put the sock cap onto his head. Finally, he waved goodbye as he followed Curtis out the door and into the parking lot.

Kim gave me a hug and decided to make fun of me. "Oh, I owe you so much!" she mocked. "Anything you need you big stud."

"Shhhh, they're going to hear you," I said. "Don't make me feel stupid. That man makes me feel some type of way, and I'm not sure what to do around him."

"I'm sorry, I was just playing," she said. "I'll see you later."

I watched as the pulled away before cleaning up my kitchen and taking a shower before bed. Once I was all clean, I climbed under my blanket, pulling it up to my chin.

As cold as it was outside, my heater was having a hard time keeping up. Once I was warmed up, I let my hand trail down the thin top I was wearing, pausing to caress my nipples.

They were already hard from being so cold, and my touch gave me goosebumps along my entire body. It would have felt even better if it had been Nick's hand touching me.

I loved having Nick in my house. I watched him the entire time he was eating, looking away anytime his glance came my way. I didn't want to seem weird or making it completely obvious that I was watching him.

I did my best to steal an odd glance here and there. While he ate, I could see the muscles under his shirt flexing without him even trying. He had a large neck that I'd love to kiss, running my tongue along to his ear and biting on his earlobe.

Out of everything I liked about him, his hands were my favorite thing about him. I don't know what it is about guys who have big hands, but they always drive me crazy.

The bigger they are, the better in my opinion. I also liked the d the fact that his hands were calloused and the skin on them was hard and leathery.

They were the hands of a worker, a man who is strong and could probably provide for his family well. I bet he could do other things well with those hands as well, especially those long, thick fingers.

I moved my hands lower down my body, rubbing them along my tummy. I may be a curvy girl, but I've always been proud of my flat stomach.

I worked hard to have my body, and I liked the way it felt when I ran my fingers over it. As I imagined Nick's hands caressing me, I allowed my hand to slip down further, rubbing myself over the top of my panties.

I teased myself, circling my clit with my middle finger. When I felt like I needed more, I pulled my panties down.

I placed my finger just inside my lips, feeling the slick, wet feeling of my pussy. I slid my finger in just enough to get it a little wet before moving it back up to my clit.

The slick lubrication allowed me to circle my clit with no resistance. I shuttered at the feeling as I slipped my finger back inside if my pussy, the feelings of pleasure running through my body.

Closing my eyes, I could imagine Nick lying there beside me, using his hand to pleasure me instead of mine. I could feel his thumb running circles around my clit while his fingers moved in and out of my hole.

I felt my climax coming quickly while I pictured Nick climbing on top of me, plunging his cock into my tight pussy. As I started to climax, I could hear Nick moaning into my ear as he filled me up at the same time.

I arched my back and bit down on my lip as I got myself off. My orgasm had been one of the best I'd had in ages. Easily as good as any orgasm a man had given me.

The thoughts of Nick were really doing something to

me. I wondered what a real orgasm with him would feel like.

The orgasm had left me spent so I rolled over onto my side, not even worried about pulling my panties back up. It didn't take me long to fall asleep and have dream after dream about him.

8
NICK

Curtis was keeping me busy with lots of work and long hours. In the last month, we'd been working so much that I'd only had two days off. That was fine with me because long hours and extra days meant big paychecks with plenty of overtime hours on them.

As the money was rolling in, I was able to get a lot of things that I really needed. It was nice to be able to finally by my own deodorant, soap, and shampoo, but it was especially nice to be able to buy any brand I wanted instead of whatever commissary decided to carry.

I didn't like the fact that Curtis had been supplying me with the things I needed, and I was grateful to be able to purchase them on my own.

Once I had the necessities, I saved every other penny I made so I could get my own set of wheels. Curtis took me all over the place, visiting many different car lots until I found what I was looking for: a black Chevy pickup truck.

The truck wasn't even close to being new, but it looked nice enough, and it ran like a dream. It didn't need any additional work and was ready to go right off the lot, which was the most important thing to me.

When I wasn't working, I killed time hanging out with Curtis and Kim. Alexa had been hanging out with us quite a bit as well. Even though I hadn't had much downtime, I'd gotten to know her quite a bit better. She even spent the holidays at the house with us.

Alexa and I had long conversations that usually continued well after our best friends went to bed. As much as I hated it, I had no choice but to lie to her about my past. She was aware that Curtis and I met in foster care, but that was all she knew about me. I hated lying to her, but what else was I supposed to do?

There was no way I could be honest with her. Not if I wanted her to actually take an interest in me and want to be with me. If she knew that I'd spent time in prison and would always be known as a former convict, she'd just view me as a fuck up and never want to speak to me again.

It wasn't like I was proud that I'd spent time in prison. As a matter of fact, I'd never been more ashamed of anything in my life.

Even though I loved spending so much time with her

at Curtis's house, it wasn't nearly enough for me. I wanted more. No, I needed more. The problem was that I was having trouble coming right out and telling her.

It wasn't like me, and I had no idea what my fucking problem was. Before I got sent to prison, I would have asked her without any hesitation. Instead, I found myself conflicted about making a move, mostly because I feared I'd never be able to show her the real me.

Even though we talked a lot and she flirted, I still wasn't sure whether or not she was as into me as I was her. There were times when it felt like she was hanging on every word that came out of my mouth or would smile while looking at me with a gleam in her gorgeous eyes.

The more I thought about it, the more I realized that there was definitely something there between us. There was almost a sort of electrical charge anything she would reach over and lightly touch my arm. I loved making her laugh because she had a smile that could melt the heart of any man, and the sound of her laughter filled the room and gave me a happy feeling that had been missing for years.

I was surprised to see Alexa sitting on the couch next to Kim when Curtis and I arrived home from work. She usually didn't come over until later in the evening.

"Hello boys," Kim joked as we took our work boots off in the foyer, so we didn't track mud through the house. "Alexa is going to have dinner with us this evening. You don't mind, do you Nick?"

I shot Kim a look that told her to shut up, and she replied with a mischievous wink. I was glad to know that Alexa was going to be having dinner with us.

"It's your food," I said laughing.

As we ate our meal, I had a hard time looking at Alexa. I worried that my window of opportunity may be closing and that if I didn't ask her out soon, I might blow it. Seeing her that night, I knew I had to make my move.

She was giving me all the right signals. She was laughing at all of my jokes, even the ones that weren't very funny. I'd catch her checking me out when she thought I wasn't paying any attention.

Once dinner was over, and everything was cleaned up, Alexa said she had to go and started telling everyone goodnight. My chance had come, and I wasn't about to let it slip by.

"Hold on just a second," I said as she put on her coat

and headed for the front door. "I'll walk you out to your car."

I snatched my coat off the hanging and clumsily threw it on.

"Okay," she replied, acting shy all of a sudden.

She gave Kim a hug and waved goodbye to Curtis. I held the door open for her and followed her out, closing it behind me.

"Dinner was delicious," she said, breaking the awkward silence that had developed as we stood next to her vehicle.

"It really was. Between you and Kim, I'm eating better lately than I've ever eaten in my life."

She smiled at the compliment, showing off a dimple in her cheek that I'd never noticed before. I looked down at the snow, trying to find the right words to say what I wanted to say. I figured the best thing to do was to spit it out and get it over with.

"So, when I was at your apartment fixing your SUV, you told me that you owe me big time. Do you remember that?"

"Yes," she laughed, looking as though she was confused as to where this conversation was going.

"I was wondering if maybe I could cash in on that," I told her.

I closed my mouth and waited to see what her reaction was before I went any further. The last thing I wanted to do was make a giant fool of myself if I had misread her signals. My heart was pounding in my chest, and she looked even more confused than she had previously.

"Um, maybe. What do you have in mind?"

"I think you should let me take you out to dinner."

Finally, it was out there. I'd asked her out, and the ball was no longer in my court. It was up to her to give me a response. I was a little nervous that her reply might not be what I wanted to hear, but at least it was all out in the open.

Alexa didn't give me an immediate answer. I studied her facial expressions, hoping to get some kind of clue of what was going on inside her head, but I couldn't read her at all.

She appeared to be surprised that I asked her out. Remaining silent, she just stood there looking at me. I could feel the smile that had formed on my face slowly beginning to disappear. I was genuinely worried that my biggest fear was about to become a reality. She was going to say no.

I knew that this was going to happen. I told myself that I would just make a fool out of myself, and there I was. I was about to tell her goodnight and go back inside when I saw her surprised look turn into a huge smile.

"When I said I owed you big time, I meant that I owed you something. Not the other way around," she told me. "How does you taking me out to dinner justify that. I'm supposed to owe you something, not the other way around. Maybe I've got a better idea."

"Okay, let's hear it."

"Why don't you come over to my place this weekend and I'll cook a special dinner just for you. How does that sound?"

Was she being serious? How does that sound? That sounded amazing. As much as I wanted to take her out and have an official first date with her, this was a much, much better idea.

Not only would I get to enjoy a meal with her, but I'd get to spend time with her alone in her apartment. Kim and Curtis wouldn't be there. It would just be her and me. In a restaurant, there was only so much that could happen between the two of us. In her apartment, though? The possibilities were endless.

The night could hold anything in store for the two of us. It would be just her and me sitting at her kitchen table. Maybe we'd sit on her couch and watch television. Hell, perhaps the two of us would even end up in bed together.

"Nick?" she asked, bringing me back to reality and alerting me to the fact that I hadn't answered her question.

"I'm sorry, yes, that sounds great. I can't wait."

"I can't wait either. How does 6:00 Saturday night sound to you?"

"That will be perfect. I'll be there," I said as I shoved my freezing hands into my coat pocket.

"Great, I'll see you then," she told me as she got into her SUV and started it up.

I stood in the driveway and watched as she drove away, not moving from my spot until I could no longer see the red from her taillights.

The amount of happiness I was feeling could not be put into words. I couldn't remember the last time I felt as happy as I did at that very moment. I wondered if I was falling in love. I'd never truly been in love before, and the feeling was foreign to me, but I had to assume that it was precisely that.

I was in love with Alexa, and it looked things might finally be starting to happen. I was finally on my way to making that woman mine.

9
NICK

The days that followed Alexa offering to cook a meal for me seemed to drag on and on. All I wanted was for Saturday to finally arrive. I spent every night that week outside of her apartment, fantasizing about how our date might go.

I played scenario after scenario in my head, yet I had no clue which of those ideas might actually play out. All I knew is that I couldn't wait for the date to actually arrive.

Everything seemed to take a lot longer than usual. Work days, which usually whizzed by since we are always so busy, dragged on.

The evenings were even worse since Alexa hadn't been back over since I asked her out. Apparently, she had something going on at work that required her to attend specialized training.

When Saturday finally arrived, I felt like I was a kid coming down the stairs to see presents under the tree on Christmas morning. I had a hard time keeping my excitement to myself.

I woke up early in the morning, barely sleeping the night before. I'd gotten home around 3:00 in the morning and only slept until about 7:00. I got up and put my energy to good use, shoveling the driveway from the massive snow that came the night before.

Even that wasn't enough to burn off the adrenaline I was feeling so I went back to my room and did a couple hundred pushups before breakfast.

I went through the clothes I'd been buying several times trying to figure out what to wear. I never understood women taking so long to get ready, but I felt like I was getting a taste of it already. I decided on a nice pair of jeans and a black and blue button-up shirt.

In the bathroom, I looked at myself in the mirror. I felt like I looked menacing, especially when I wasn't smiling. A scary looking man was who I always saw when I looked into the mirror.

I hadn't scared Alexa off, however.

It was like she could see deep inside of me and see the good man that was inside. Besides, I never frown when I'm around Alexa. She always kept me laughing and smiling. I'm sure that had a lot to do with it.

I took the clothes off and sat them down on the bed, making sure not to wrinkle them. Still having more energy to burn off, I dropped to the floor and did more pushups.

It was something I did a lot in prison, and some habits are hard to break. Once I was done, I jumped in the shower before completely shaving my face, the first time I'd done it since going to prison.

As soon as I was done, I looked at myself in the mirror and regretted my decision. I looked like a different person. I looked like I was ten years younger than I actually was. I didn't even recognize myself.

What is the matter with you? Alexa's going to think you look like a child. Fuck man, you've ruined everything!

I stood in the bathroom for nearly an hour, just staring at myself in the mirror. Shaving off my facial hair was leaving me a lot more stressed than it should have.

I kept telling myself how stupid I was as I paced back and forth, the walls feeling as though they were closing in on me. In a way, it felt like I was back in prison.

Eventually, I was able to calm myself down. There was no way to know in advance how she was going to react to my new look. For all I knew, she'd like it a lot and me stressing over it would be all for nothing. Before I knew it, it was time for me to go.

I got dressed, threw a little gel in my hair, sprayed on some cologne that I'd bought and left the house. I didn't want to show up empty-handed, so I stopped at a little grocery store and picked up a small bouquet of flowers before continuing on to her apartment.

My nerves were pretty much shot. My heart was pounding much harder than I'd ever known it to pound before.

I felt anxious and just wanted to get there so we could get the date started. I was feeling nervous and excited at the same time. By the time I made it to her door, I knew I had to get myself under control. I breathed in and out slowly until my heart rate was back to normal. After one more deep breath, I knocked on the door.

It was tough to control my breathing, but I did the best I could. I just focused on the flowers in my hand and hoped for the best. I heard her rushing up to the door before it opened and she was standing there looking back at me.

Somehow, she was even more beautiful than the last time I saw her. I've always thought she looked good, but that night, she looked better than I'd ever seen her.

I looked her up and down, drinking in how perfect she was. She was wearing a pair of jeans that hugged her body perfectly.

The sweater she was wearing was snug but still loose enough to leave some things to the imagination. Her face was glowing, and her cheeks appeared to be a little flushed.

She may have been nervous, or it could have had something to do with her makeup. Regardless of which it was, I loved the way it looked on her.

"Hey there," she said as she smiled at me and held the door open for me. "Come on in," she requested as she looked over my face before turning her attention to the flowers in my hand.

Alexa stepped out of the way, allowing me to enter her apartment.

"I stopped and got these for you," I told her as held the flowers in front of her face.

Real smooth, jackass.

"Thank you so much, Nick! They're gorgeous. I love them," she gushed as she marched straight into the kitchen and pulled a vase out of a cabinet.

I stood just inside her front door, unsure of where I was supposed to go or what I should do next. I knew I didn't want to track snow through her apartment so I kicked my shoes off and sat them next to the door. Alexa was putting water in the vase when she noticed I was still standing there like an idiot.

"What are you doing? Come on in here," she waved her hand at me.

Not knowing what to say, I just nodded my head and

made my way into the kitchen. Alexa kept looking at me, paying close attention to my face.

"I can't believe how different you look with your face completely shaved," she said with a smile.

"Yeah, I really don't know what I was thinking. It looks terrible," I said, rubbing my hands along where my beard had been earlier that day.

"What are you talking about? I love it. You look so good. I mean, I liked the beard too, but I really like this."

I smiled, finally feeling like shaving wasn't a mistake.

"What is this?" she asked, scanning my face. "Is that a dimple I see? It is!"

Alexa reached up and ran her hand along my cheek. Her sudden touch made me freeze up, my entire body becoming stiff under her touch.

It was a reflex that I'd developed in prison. Just as soon as I froze up, I allowed myself to relax, leaning my head against her hand.

As soon as I felt her hand on my face, it was gone. She'd jerked her hand away. She smiled an uncomfortable smile at me and turned towards the kitchen table.

The table was already set for the fantastic meal that she prepared for the two of us.

"Damn, I know I'm a big guy but why'd you make so much food?" I joked.

"I don't know. I wasn't sure what you liked, so I kind of made a little bit of everything."

The two of us shared a laugh at her reasoning as we sat down to eat. I couldn't believe how good everything tasted. She made all kinds of foods. Some things were fried while others had been baked in the oven.

There were some items that she didn't even know what they were. She just followed recipes she'd found online. Eventually, she told me that she searched what to make for a dinner date at home and ended up on Pinterest.

"Pinterest? What's Pinterest?" I asked her.

"You don't know what Pinterest is?" Alexa joked, thinking I was pulling her leg.

"I have no clue. Is it like a cookbook or something?"

"Have you been living under some kind of rock? Pinterest is a website where people share their favorite things. In this instance, I was searching for recipes and, as you can see, found way too many."

I nodded, acting like I knew what she was talking about. Even before I went to prison, I wasn't exactly too big on computers.

Still, I figured I better be careful, or she may start to question why I didn't seem to know much about anything that had become popular in the last five years.

The two of us continued to eat while talking and

laughing the entire time. When the meal was over, I helped her clear the plate and wash up the dishes.

"You don't have to do that," she said. "You're my guest. Why don't you go have a seat while I finish this up?"

"No way. After the great meal you prepared, this is the least I can do. I insist."

"Okay then, I appreciate it very much. I just hope you saved a little room. There's a few dessert options for later."

Dessert options? Was she saying what I thought she was saying?

"What kind of options?" I asked, hoping I already knew the answer.

"I whipped up a few things. They're all chilling in the fridge for now. They should be ready in the next hour or so."

Damn. I was way off on that one.

After we were done cleaning up from our meal, we moved the conversation into her living room. She sat on one end of the couch, and I sat on the other, our bodies turned inward towards one another.

I leaned back, resting my arm on the back of the couch while she sat with her legs folded under herself. As we talked, I noticed that she had a habit of running her fingers through her hair.

She only did it when she was the one doing the talking. It had to be some kind of nervous reaction. Whatever the case, I liked it.

I made sure to control the conversation, not wanting to give her many opportunities to ask me about my past. She told me about her job and the fact that, while she hates working in a convenience store, the money she'll make once she advances will more than make up for it.

I learned that she wasn't close to any members of her family, but didn't press the issue. I'd love to know why, especially if there was a chance that we could both have a similarly fucked up background but that would just lead to more questions asked of me.

Before either of us knew it, we'd been sitting on the couch for hours. Those hours felt like minutes. I felt so comfortable with her. It was a feeling that I'd never felt with anyone else before. When I was with her, I was happy. Everything felt right.

"I don't mean to sound sappy or anything, but I'm really glad we were able to get together tonight," she told me, and she smiled and looked into my eyes.

"I am too. This has been really nice," I replied, shifting my position just a bit to move in a little closer to her.

Alexa Kind of looked me up and down and smiled at me.

Shit, I didn't take that one as smooth as I should have.

"So, you ready for some dessert?" she asked.

There was something about the way she'd just asked me the question. She spoke in a hushed tone, her breathing a little heavier than it had been. She blinked at me as she waited for an answer, her eyes looking as though they were being weighed down in anticipation.

I could feel the ache inside of me getting stronger. It was a feeling that I'd had from the moment I stepped into the apartment, but now that we were sitting right next to each other, it was getting to be more than I could take. While Alexa involuntarily licked her lips, I let out a deep breath and shook my head up and down.

I was well aware that any discussion about food was out the window. I looked her in the eyes, neither of us blinking.

Alexa smiled a nervous smile before biting her bottom lip. Making sure to move much more smoothly than earlier, I maneuvered myself even closer to her.

I could see the excitement in the sparkles of her eyes. I felt like, for the first time since we'd met, that she wanted just as much as I wanted her.

I leaned in closer to her, cupping her face with my hand and using my fingertips to lightly rub into her neck. Alexa exhaled and leaned into my touch.

I knew that this was my chance and wasn't about to let it pass by. I brought her face to mine and gently kissed her lips. Her lips were soft, and it felt like they were made to kiss mine.

The second kiss was harder, causing Alexa to open her mouth. Taking my top lip between hers, she gave it a slight tug and a little bit of a suck. I moaned, even though I hadn't intended to.

Alexa began to take control as she grabbed me by the side of my face and pulled me in closer to her. Our kisses got heavier, and I started using my tongue more and more, dipping it into her mouth, licking her lips and caressing her tongue with mine. She made soft whimpering noises, which had me rock hard in a matter of seconds.

Her hands grabbed at my hair, pulling me in closer and closer. Before I knew it, I was completely leaned over the top of her body with her lying down on the couch beneath me, her legs wrapped around my waist. I moved with her, slowly lowering myself down on top of her.

After weeks and weeks of fantasizing about her, it was finally happening. I wanted to be as close to her as I possibly could be.

I also knew that I was a big guy so I had to use my arm to brace my bodyweight so I wouldn't crush. Supporting myself using the back of the couch, I pushed my hips into hers, using my hands to feel around the curves of her body.

For a curvy girl, her body was tight as hell. I ran my

hand all the way around to her ass, grabbing a handful and pulling her into me.

I stopped for a moment and looked her in the eyes. Before I took things any further, I wanted to be sure we were on the same page.

I remembered Curtis telling me that she was a good girl. Even as bad as I wanted her, I wanted to make sure she wanted me in the same ways. I didn't want to go too far too fast and ruin things before anything even got started.

Alexa's eyes were filled to the brim with lust and desire. The look she gave me seemed to burn straight through to my soul. The look on her face made me freeze and took it in, her beauty having an effect on me. Before I knew what hit me, she grabbed me by my hair and pulled me to her.

I felt like I was an awkward preteen, fumbling with my hands as I pawed at her breasts through the sweater she was wearing.

While we kissed sloppily, I moved my hand down between her legs, turning it just right to be able to press against her sweet spot, providing just a bit of pressure. She gasped in between kisses, making me apply even more pressure before grabbing the top of her jeans and tugging them downward.

Alexa cooperated, arching her body and allowing me

to remove them and toss them to the side of the couch.

With her jeans discarded, I traced my hand up the inside of her thigh, feeling her soft skin and watching as goosebumps appeared beneath my soft touch.

Making my way up, I rubbed softly through her panties. Alexa was already unbelievably wet. It was very apparent even through the soft material. I could also feel the heat radiating from her.

She was moving her hips as I touched her, so I continued, this time dipping my fingers inside of her panties. I was pleased to find that she was as completely shaven. I ran my fingers down to her clit and started rubbing in a circular motion.

Alexa moaned loudly as I looked down at her. She looked hot as hell lying there with her eyes closed, biting her bottom lip.

I rubbed her in a circular motion while using my middle finger to stroke at her pussy lips. They were so soft and warm. As they spread for my fingers, her wetness engulfed my finger, allowing it to sink into her easily.

I loved the way her pussy engulfed my finger, squeezing tightly on it. I could only imagine how much it would squeeze my cock.

Alexa was completely at my mercy as I alternated fucking her with my finger and pulling it out and using it to rub her clit. It didn't take long before her labored breathing got even harder and she climaxed for me.

As tight as she had been before, her orgasm only caused her to clamp down even more on my finger. She arched her back and pushed her pelvis against my hand, moaning to herself as her legs began to shake.

When she came down from her orgasmic high, I slowly removed my finger from within her. I had to fight the urge to lick her juices off my finger, afraid that doing so would make her think I was some kind of weirdo or creep. Instead, I just looked down at her, waiting to see what was going to happen next.

Her eyes were still closed, and I had no clue what I was supposed to say to her at that point. Eventually, she opened her eyes a smiled an embarrassed smile in my direction.

"Are you good?" I asked her, realizing that maybe it wasn't the best choice of words at that moment.

I just didn't want her to regret what had just happened between us. I was concerned that maybe I'd moved too fast for her. Had it been too much too soon? I was getting worried until she smiled and looked up at me.

"Yeah, I'm good," she replied, her smile suddenly turning into a bit of a frown. "It's just that I really don't want to stop," she confided in me, looking up to gauge my reaction. Apparently, she was worried about the same thing I was.

"Nobody said we had to stop anything baby girl," I stated with a chuckle as I moved my hands up to her hips and wrapped my arms around her.

I needed her more than I even realized. I lifted her up off the couch, allowing her to wrap her legs around my waist while kissing my neck and I carried her from the living room to the bedroom.

Alexa slid off me and had me sit down on the edge of her bed while she slowly removed her shirt. I was in awe of how amazing she looked standing there in nothing but her panties and bra. I soaked up the view of her body, taking it all in as though I was trying to commit it to my memory.

In my opinion, her body was the very definition of perfection. I could see that she took care of herself. Her body had good muscle tone while being curvy at the same time. She was firm and tight but supple and soft in all the areas that really mattered.

With a soft touch, I ran my hand along her waist, enjoying the feeling of her curvy hips. I ran my hand even further down her thigh before bending down to kiss her stomach.

I couldn't get enough of the soft, smooth feel of her body. She also smelled so good. Her scent was sweet, kind of like fresh flowers. Alexa pushed me backward and began pulling my shirt up and over my head.

Standing up off the bed, she looked tiny lying there under my large frame. She reached up to me, running her hands up and down over my chest, feeling my muscles, before trailing her fingers down towards my stomach and continuing until she reached my belt.

Using it as leverage, she pulled me in close to her and began kissing my chest. The feeling turned me on even more than I already was, causing me to grab her by the hair.

She continued kissing along my chest, stopping to lick on my nipple, alternating her kisses with light nibbles. Before I knew what was happening, she had my belt undone and my zipper down.

Alexa tugged on my pants, trying to pull them down. She wasn't making much progress, so I helped her by yanking them down myself and tossing them on the floor next to the bed.

When I looked up, I was able to follow her eyes as she was staring at my cock poking through my boxers. My erection was standing straight out, looking like it was trying to break through the barrier of my underwear. Alexa didn't waste another second.

She slid her hand into my boxers and pulled them down past my knees, where I finished kicking them off onto the floor. With a hand firmly planted on my chest, she pushed me down onto the bed, where I sat, watching as she slid her panties off and unclasped her bra.

She had perfect tits. They were high and perky. My favorite thing about them was the way they jiggled slightly with each move she made.

As she approached me, I grabbed her by the waist and pulled her into me, taking one of her breasts into my mouth. I flicked my tongue over her hardened nipple while I listened to her moaning into my ear. I loved the sounds she made when I was pleasuring her.

She braced herself by placing both of her hands on my shoulder. Every flick of my tongue made her moan a little more. Every soft kiss on her skin was met with a sigh. Each touch I placed on her body made her whimper with pleasure.

I enjoyed the effect I was having on her. She had no idea how bad I'd wanted this. I had a feeling it was going to be good, but I had no clue just how good it was going to be.

My body felt like it was going to explode in anticipation. I couldn't wait any longer. I moved my hands to her back and run them down until I reached her backside.

She had a fantastic ass. It was high and round, just the way I liked it. I continued kissing, licking, and nibbling on her nipples as I squeezed her ass and pulled her body towards me until she straddled me.

Alexa grabbed my shoulders for support as she raised her ass up and slid her pussy slowly down onto my cock. I tried to play it cool but I couldn't. I let out a loud groan as the sensation of her slowly sliding down onto me became too much to handle.

I couldn't believe how tight she was. Her pussy felt amazing wrapped around me like a glove. I wrapped my arms around her and pressed my head against her body, closing my eyes and enjoying the sensation of her moving up and down on me.

She started off by riding me slowly, almost as though she was trying to tease me. I could feel a frenzy starting to build deep inside my body.

As good as she felt on top of me, I wanted more. I wanted to take her harder and faster. I wanted to pound her hard and show her what it was like to be taken by a real man.

Reaching around her body, I lifted her up, turned my body, and tossed her onto the bed. I positioned myself at the side of the bed between her legs and watched as she opened them for me with no hesitation.

I grabbed her legs and entered her, starting off slowly, letting her feel every inch of me sliding into her body. As soon as I was pushed into her as deep as I would go, I leaned down and kissed her deeply.

Alexa wrapped her arms around my neck, moving her hands up and down over the muscles in my back as I pushed myself in and out of her. Her moans became louder and louder until they transformed into uncontrolled screams.

She was losing herself in me just like I was losing myself in her. We were getting lost in one another. This was precisely what I'd wanted since the day I met her. I wanted to show her that I was different. I wanted to make her feel things that no other man had ever been able to make her feel.

I started pumping into her harder and faster, her pussy squeezing my dick tightly. Her legs clamped down around my waist, and her grip on my neck tightened. She screamed loudly as the pleasure of another orgasm took over her.

The sound of her screams and the feeling of her cumming was too much for me to take. I pushed her down onto the bed and emptied myself into her. All of my weight was on her as my dick continued pumping. I came for what felt like forever until I made one last big thrust into her before allowing my body to relax.

I felt the beads of sweat on my forehead and tried to control my breathing, but I felt like I'd just had the best workout of my life. I slowly pulled myself out of her and moved over to her side.

Both of us were out of breath and completely unable to talk. Instead, we both laid together, each of us completely satisfied in ways that we'd never experienced before. I'd finally gotten what I'd been wanting more than anything in the world, and this was only the start of things to come. She was going to be mine from then until the end of time. I just knew it.

10
NICK

The weeks that followed our first time together were some of the best weeks I'd ever had in my life. I couldn't remember a single time when I'd ever been happier.

Of course, with everything that's gone down in my life, it wasn't tough to say that, but I had a feeling that even if I'd had a perfect life up until that point, I still would have felt the same way.

Whenever I was with her, nothing else seemed to matter. Life felt perfect.

The two of us were spending nearly every day together. When I wasn't working, I was at her place. Most of our time together was spent in bed, but I was more than okay with that.

We spent the holidays with Curtis and Kim,

exchanging a few small gifts and having the first real holiday meal I'd ever had. It was by the far the best Christmas of my life.

As Alexa and I spent more and more time together, I was really able to get to know her well. The more I got to know her, the more I realized what a great person she was.

Not only was she gorgeous but she was also the kindest person I'd ever encountered. On top of that, she was a hell of a lot of fun. She was someone I could be completely silly with, and I loved that.

We were always making each other laugh. She was also so caring and generous. No matter what she was feeling or doing, she always made sure that I was happy and completely satisfied in every way.

Being with someone like her was strange. I'd never had the opportunity the be with someone that I wanted to treat so well and I sure as hell had never been with someone who treated me the way she was treating me.

Women in the past just wanted what they wanted, and that was the end of it. Sure, they all wanted different things but in the end, they were all the same. Not one woman I'd ever been with put me first.

When it came to wants and needs, mine were always an afterthought. Nobody had ever cared about what I thought. That's why Alexa was different. She made me feel like I actually had value. She made me feel like I mattered.

I'd already had strong feelings for her to begin with. Even when I didn't know her that well, I knew there was something about her that I wanted to know.

Now that I knew her on a much deeper and intimate level, I felt as though I couldn't get enough of her. During the rare times we weren't together, I wasn't able to get her off my mind. I hated being away from her.

When Alexa and I weren't together, I couldn't turn my mind off and couldn't help but let my insecurities get the better of me.

No matter how hard I tried to fight them off, the bad thoughts would always come back to cloud my mind. Did she really feel the same about me as I felt about her?

Neither of us had said I love you to the other. Was it too soon for that? Would that freak her out? I definitely felt it for her. Why hadn't she said it to me? The only thing I could think of was that she didn't feel the same way. When we weren't together, was she with somebody else? Did she wake up one morning and realize she could do better than me?

That was the thing about her and I. Even though I was falling hard for her and wanted her more than anything, I was smart enough to know that I didn't actually deserve a girl like her.

She was way out of my league.

A woman like Alexa deserved the best out of life. She deserved to be with someone who had loads of money and could give her flowers and jewelry on a regular basis. She deserved someone who could take her on trips to lavish and luxurious places. She deserved someone who could give her anything and everything she could ever possibly want.

I knew that, when it came to most of those things, I wouldn't be able to give her what she deserved. No matter how hard I worked, I was going to be stuck working construction for the rest of my life.

My criminal record would ensure that most of the better-paying jobs would stay out of reach for me. I had to put the thought of my criminal record coming to light out of my mind.

I hoped that Alexa would never come to find out about my record because if she did, I had serious doubts that she would love me enough to not care about the trouble I'd been into.

After I was able to buy my truck, I was saving most of my money to get a place of my own. Finally, the day came when I was able to move out of the room Curtis had been letting me stay in and into my own place.

The apartment wasn't anything to write home about.

It was a pretty small studio apartment on the wrong side of town, but it was mine.

It was cheap, and it included most of the utilities, so I didn't have much to complain about. I didn't plan on being there all that often anyway.

When I wasn't at work, I was usually with Alexa so the apartment would be empty most of the time. Still, it was going to be nice to have a space of my own when we couldn't be together.

Work had been particularly hard for about a week, and I was looking forward to getting off. I had plans for the evening.

I was going to swing by my place, take a hot shower, and meet Alexa for dinner. I'd found a button that said "If it doesn't scan, it is NOT free" and I couldn't wait to give it to her.

It was a great cashier pun, and I thought it would go great with the buttons she wore on her vest when she was on cashier duty. I hoped she'd like it.

Those were the kinds of gifts I was able to give her. It wasn't expensive by any means. As the day went on, I started to develop a bit of a complex about it.

What was I going to do if she didn't like what I got her?

What if she saw the small box it had come in and was

hoping that it was something else. Maybe she expected it to be something nice like jewelry. Was she going to be disappointed? The last thing I wanted to do was disappoint her.

By the time I was clocking out at work, my mind was spiraling into madness. I wished I could turn my brain off when it came to over thinking but I couldn't. It was something I couldn't help.

When I got to the parking lot at her apartment, I debated whether or not I should give her the button. Eventually, I grabbed it out of the truck and made my way inside.

When I entered her apartment, I found Alexa sprawled out on the couch, enjoying one of the romance novels she liked to read. Before the door was even closed behind me, she'd already jumped off the sofa and ran over to me for a hug. She wrapped her arms around my waist and rested her chin on my chest, looking up at me with the biggest smile on her face.

"Hey you," she said as she looked up at me.

She had an adoring look in her eyes. Whenever she looked at me like that, all the doubt and insecurity flew out the window.

That look made me realize how ridiculous I was forever questioning her feelings about me. I grabbed her by both sides of the face and gave her a soft kiss on the lips.

"Hi baby," I whispered to her as I ran my hands through her hair.

I leaned in a little closer and gave her a kiss on her forehead. As always, she smelled fantastic. I loved standing there, inhaling her scent as I held her in her arms.

"Is everything okay?" she asked.

I was a bit surprised by the sudden concern in her voice and her face as she pulled back a bit to look up at me.

"Yeah, I'm good. It's just been a rough week at work."

I followed her into the kitchen, grabbing a bottle of beer from the fridge while she jumped up on the counter and started telling me about her day at work.

I always thought it was cute how much she seemed to love her job. I wished I was able to be so enthusiastic about mine. Her eyes lit up when she talked about one of her co-workers or some of her regular customers.

Since she was already talking about her job, I figured it would be the perfect time to give her the gift I'd brought for her. I pulled the small red box out of my pocket and stood right in front of her, holding it out for her to grab.

"I saw this the other day, and I wanted you to have it," I told her. She smiled as she took it out of my hand, apparently not expecting me to bring her a gift.

My stomach was twisting and turning itself into knots

as she opened the box. I remember thinking how ridiculous it was to be getting myself so worked up over something as simple as a button.

"It's not much really," I continued. "I hope you like it."

Alexa slid the top of the box off, and I studied her face, waiting to see what kind of a reaction my gift was going to induce.

She looked down and smiled as she read it before she started laughing out loud. The sound of her laughter was a welcome one. She grabbed my shoulder with one hand as she leaned in to give me a kiss. When she pulled away, she still had a smile on her face.

"Where in the world did you find this?" she asked. "I love it. I'm pretty sure it's my new favorite button," she told me as she grabbed her vest from the back of the chair next to us and pinned it to it. "Thank you so much. I can't wait to wear it at work. You have no clue how many times a day someone makes that dumb joke to me. Maybe the button will make them think twice." She gave me another hug and a kiss.

"You really like it that much?" I asked her.

"Yes, silly. I love it. You know how I am about my buttons. I love this one because it's personal and thoughtful. Oh, and because it's from you."

Even though she seemed happy and thankful, I

couldn't help but feel stupid about the fact that I'd given it to her at all. Instead of making me happy that I'd given her a gift, I just felt like an idiot. Alexa had never done anything to act like a materialistic person, and I knew she wasn't, but that wasn't the point.

"I don't know," I started. "I guess I feel like I should have gotten you something better. You are the best thing that has ever happened to me, and if I buy you a gift, it should be better than a three-dollar button," I exclaimed, taking a step back and looking down at the floor.

"Where is this coming from Nick?" Alexa asked, surprised at the way I was acting. I knew she didn't care about the price. She seemed to actually like the button a lot. "I want you to stop thinking that way. I love the button a lot," she said as she grabbed my shirt and pulled me back towards her. Her hands began to wander, running over my chest and causing my muscles to tense up under her touch. "It was very sweet," she told me, running her hands up to my face, letting her fingers skip over my stubble.

"I don't know, Alexa. I just can't get over the feeling that I'm not good enough for you," I blurted out. As surprised as she looked, I was even more surprised that I said what I'd been feeling out loud. Alexa's eyes were wide, and the expression on her face made it seem like I'd just hurt her badly.

"What would make you say something like that to me?" she asked with her eyebrows furrowed at me, visibly upset by what I'd said.

"Well, it's just that you're so," I began, not sure where I was actually going before I opened my mouth. The thing was, I never even meant to say what I said. Yeah, those were my thoughts but I sure as hell never intended to let her know about it. Now I was even more worried because she'd know how fucked up my way of thinking was. "You're so perfect," I continued. "You're so beautiful and sexy and just perfect while I'm pretty much a nobody. I have no clue what I even have to offer you."

When I looked up at her, she had the saddest look in her eyes that I'd ever seen. I knew right then and there that I shouldn't have said anything.

"Nick, I don't ever want you to think that way. Believe me, I am far from perfect. As for you, don't ever refer to yourself as a nobody. The time that we've spent together since we met has been nothing short of amazing. You're one of the sweetest men I've ever met."

Alexa pulled me in closer to her, getting rid of any space between the two of us. She wanted to make sure I understood what her feelings were.

"You're so fun to be around," she continued. "You're so funny. You keep me laughing all the time. You are a gorgeous man. You make me happier than anyone has made me in a long time. I love the things you say to me. I love the things you do to me. I love the way you touch me."

From out of nowhere, she grabbed my hand and put it between her legs. I took the hint and started rubbing her through the sweatpants she had on. She leaned into, giving me a soft kiss before moving her mouth to my ear.

"I love you, Nick," she whispered.

Time seemed to stand still as I heard those words come out of her mouth. My mind raced, and I thought that my heart actually stopped until I realized that I could hear it pounding in my chest.

My chest tightened, and my stomach felt like it was twisted into knots. My head was spinning as I stared at her, unable to respond. I watched as Alexa inhaled, waiting for some kind of reply from me.

I could tell that she was getting nervous. I was sure she thought that she couldn't take back what she said.

"You do?" Yeah, those were the two words I managed to choke out of my mouth. Alexa smiled a bit and nodded her head up and down. "I love you so much," was my response to her as I began kissing her neck lightly, allowing the happiness of the moment and the joy in her words take over.

I grabbed Alexa and lifted her off the counter and to the floor. Taking her by the hand, I led her into her bedroom where I laid her down on the bed and pulled her sweatpants and panties right off of her body.

She sat up and took off her top. She hadn't been wearing a bra, so her breasts jiggled with her movements. I couldn't look away from her as I was reminded once again just how lucky I was. I looked her up and down, making sure to pause and get a better look at my favorite parts of her body.

Eventually, I met her gaze, and we began to kiss with me leaning into her, ensuring that she was going to lie back down on the bed.

My kisses were all over the place. They began on her sweet, soft, succulent lips before making their way to her neck and then down to her collarbone.

Her body shook slightly as I kissed her there, having recently learned that it was her favorite place to get kisses. Alexa whispered my name as I moved my hand to her inner thigh, caressing it gently. I wanted to tease her for a bit, much in the same way that she teased me during our first night together.

I wanted the anticipation to build. I wanted to make sure she was as wet as she could be before I made my next move. I wanted to hear her begging me for my cock. I wanted to listen to her telling me that she loved me over and over again.

From her neck, I moved down her body, kissing my

way down. When I reached her tits, I took a moment to lick and suck on them. I made sure to take my time, enjoying every second of what I was doing.

I loved the feeling of her skin. I loved the way her nipple got hard every time I ran my tongue around it. I loved the way her entire body arched up when I lightly nibbled on her sensitive skin.

"Take me, Nick," she moaned into my ear, her fingers grabbing onto my hair as I continued to suck and lick on her nipples.

I could tell that Alexa was getting close to her breaking point. She wanted me. She needed me badly. I thought back to what she'd said to me just a few minutes before. She loved me. Damn, it felt so good to hear her say those words.

Listening to her moan my name and beg for me to take her made me happy. I loved the effect I had on her. The way she wanted me was amazing. I knew it would never get old. Every single time I was with her, it still surprised me. It also excited me and made me rock hard.

I moved from her breasts and made my way down to her stomach, running my tongue along her soft, smooth skin. I kept moving south to her pelvis and towards the inner parts of her legs.

She groaned, almost growling at me. The sound was

filled with raw desire. I was getting a kick out of teasing her and hearing how much she wanted me inside of her.

Sliding down, I knelt down on the floor next to the bed. With my arms wrapped under her thighs, I pulled her to the edge. Her pussy was just inches from my face, her lips shiny and glistening with her wetness, her clit was perfectly pink and swollen with desire.

I wasn't ready to stop teasing her just yet, so I took a single finger and ran it up and down across her pussy, allowing it to lightly touch her clit for only a moment. Alexa made a gasping sound when I touched her there while she pulled my hair, trying to direct my face towards her wetness. To give her a little taste of what was to come, I slid my finger down inside of her slit and slipped it inside of her.

She was so wet that it slid right in. As I massaged her insides, I could feel her muscles tensing around my finger. It was a feeling I could never get enough of.

With my finger still inside of her, I lowered my head and flicked at her clit with my tongue, looking up at her to watch what her reaction would be.

She had her eyes closed tightly while her body wiggled around. I nibbled on her clit before sucking it into my mouth and biting on it. It was something I'd done before, and it always drove her crazy.

At the same time, I kept working my finger in and out

of her. As I could feel her getting closer, I slid another finger into her pussy.

I was all over her, sucking her clit, keeping my fingers busy inside her and using my free hand to caress and pinch at her nipple.

She loved being touched, and as her breathing started to get heavier and more shallow, I realized she was getting close. Pulling my fingers out of her, I spread her legs apart and pulled her even closer to me.

I dipped my tongue inside of her beautiful womanhood before making long strokes upward towards her clit. Alexa gasped at the sensation, and within seconds, she was cumming all over my face.

Although her legs were shaking, she arched her back and brought her pussy up to my face, leading me to dive back in for more as she wrapped her legs around my neck. I could feel her orgasm through her legs as she shivered and shook. I continued licking her pussy, lapping up as much of her sweet juices as I could.

I couldn't get enough of the way she tasted. I loved it. I continued licking and sucking as she came over and over, each orgasm seeming to be more intense than the last.

When Alexa couldn't take it anymore, she squeezed her legs tighter around my neck and did everything she could to push my head away.

She always got extra sensitive after she came a few

times. I got in one last lick as she cried out in a combination of ecstasy and agony.

She may have gotten off really well, but I wasn't even close to done with her yet. Alexa was still breathing heavily as I crawled up onto her, straddling her and kissing her neck.

She reached down, yanking at my pants, already wanting more of what I had to offer her. My cock sprang to attention as she tried everything she could to get me out of my clothes. I finally decided to help her so I stood up and undressed as fast as I could.

As soon as I crawled back on top of her, she wrapped her legs around my waist, pulling me into her. She was so slick from what I'd been doing to her that I was able to slip into her easily.

I could never get enough of how she felt when her tight pussy grabbed onto my dick. She felt amazing as I slowly pushed myself into her before pumping in and out of her. Alexa moaned as I picked up speed.

"I love you," I told her, looking into her eyes as I moved in and out of her. The words lit a passion in me. I didn't want to just tell her. I wanted her to feel just how much I loved her, so I began thrusting even deeper. "I love you," I said again.

"I love you too," Alexa said with a whimper, barely able to get the words out between moans of pleasure.

I loved the way the words sounded coming out of her mouth. As I picked up speed, I delivered the last few thrusts I had in me as I released into her. My moan was deep and primal.

I pushed her down into the mattress while her legs squeezed around me before I collapsed to her side. We both laid there, neither one of us able to catch our breath.

Sexually, I believed that Alexa and I were meant for one another. We fit together like a glove, and I'd never experienced such passion with anyone else.

Up until that point, the day Alexa said she loved me was easily the best day of my life. Of course, every day felt like that to me.

Whenever I thought it couldn't get any better, she would surprise me and prove me wrong.

I had no clue how anything would top that day. All I knew was that I loved her, and she loved me. They weren't just words. She really meant what she'd said. We loved each other, and nothing was going to take that from me. Ever.

I'd kill someone before I'd ever let that happen.

11
NICK

As winter turned into spring and spring started to make way for summer, Alexa and I did nothing but grow closer and closer to one another. By the time June rolled around, we'd been together officially for just about six months.

"You know, June is my anniversary at work, right?" she asked me.

"No, I didn't know that. Are they gonna throw you a party or something?"

"Yeah, right. Those cheapskates? I'd be surprised if the owners threw birthday parties for their own kids," she joked. "I do have some good news, though."

"What's that?"

"When my work anniversary gets here, I'll qualify for the top-tier vacation schedule."

"What does that mean?"

"It means my vacation days will be maxed. I'll have a total of twenty vacation days to use for the year on top of my personal days."

"That's awesome. Congratulations."

"Thanks! I thought that we should probably put the vacation days to good use. We should get out of here and go do something."

The two of us discussed at length what kinds of things we'd like to do. We didn't have a particular idea in mind, but we both liked a lot of the same things. We both loved nature and wanted to be outdoors. After some research, we found some cabins in Ely that looked like they'd be good to spend some time at.

Her store was going through inventory and other important things so it was going to be a few weeks before she could use any of her time off but that gave us a little bit of time to plan.

Neither of us had a ton of extra money, but when we put it together, we were able to rent a cabin for the summer. It wouldn't be ours all summer, we had no way to be able to afford that.

Instead, the rental was a shared cabin. We'd have access to it on the first week of every month.

Even though we both loved the outdoors, neither of us

had ever rented a cabin before. Hell, I'd never even been camping.

Foster homes don't really take you out to do a lot of things like that. Since it was going to be a new experience for us, we were both very excited. The cabin itself was very secluded. It was located deep in the woods. There were neighbors for miles.

There was also no television and no cell phone reception. It would just be Alexa and me with no interruptions and no distractions. That was what I liked the most about it.

No matter how much time I spent with her, I always wanted more. It never seemed like I was able to get enough of her. The last thing I wanted to do was smother her, but at the same time, I hated every second we were apart.

I never said anything when Alexa would spend the day shopping with Kim or when she wanted to set up double dates with her friends. I didn't want to be the kind of guy who complained about stuff like that, even though I didn't like to share her.

I wanted to have her all to myself. She was my girl, and I valued the time we spent together.

Alexa got to see a side of me that I kept hidden from the outside world. She got to see a side of me that I never let anyone else see, not even Curtis.

Over the months that we'd been together, I found myself opening up to her more than I ever imagined I would. I opened up about some parts of my past, but not about anything significant.

There were still some things I wasn't comfortable talking about.

I stuck to partial truths as opposed to outright lies. I gave bits and pieces of my history that actually happened, but I either gave them to her out of context, or I completely left out the more painful parts.

Even though I didn't want her to know how shitty my life had been, I hated having to lie to her. I wanted to be able to tell her about all the things that had happened to me as well as what I'd done and where I'd been for five years before I met her. It drove me insane to have to lie to her on a daily basis but what else was I supposed to do?

I had everything that I wanted. I had the love of my dream girl. I had a good job that paid the bills. Even though it wasn't the best, I had a place of my own. I was happy for the first time in my life, and I wasn't going to fuck it all up by telling Alexa about a past that I wished I could forget.

What would be the point of saying anything?

The past is over, and it's best to leave it in the rearview mirror. The things that had happened to me. The things that I'd done. They were all over. There was no going back and changing anything so why would it make sense to dwell on them. I was focused on the future, and to me, that future was all about Alexa and me.

That girl was my life. If I hadn't met her, I had no clue where I'd be. I had no idea who'd I'd be. Just thinking about that scared me and I didn't want to find out the answers to those questions.

I was waiting impatiently inside of Alexa's apartment, waiting for her to come home from work. I paced back and forth and time seemed to move incredibly slowly.

It was something I seemed to do a lot, primarily when I was either nervous or excited. I couldn't sit still. I needed to keep moving. I was definitely excited.

While I waited, I packed a bag for each of us so we were ready to leave for our week in the cabin. I didn't have to pack a whole lot. I packed some clothes, although I didn't plan on either one of us wearing them all that often.

In my mind, ahead of us was a week full of sex with food in between. Alexa had mentioned that she wouldn't mind going on a hike since we'd be out in the woods. It was something I'd never done, and it sounded cool so I agreed.

I made sure we both had the right clothes for that adventure. As I was zipping up my duffel bag, I heard the front door closing. My girl was finally there.

"Nick? Are you here?" she yelled out from the living room.

"Yeah, I'm in the bedroom," I replied.

12
ALEXA

I walked in and was surprised to see that he had everything packed and ready for the trip.

"You didn't have to do all this," I said. "I would have helped you when I got here."

"I know you would have. I was just trying to make things easier for you. I figured we could get on the road quicker if it were done." "Well, thank you," I told him as I walked up and gave him a kiss. "Let me get a quick shower, and then we can be on our way."

"That sounds good. Mind if I join you?"

"Not at all," I winked.

Nick jumped into the shower with me, soaping me up and talking about how much fun we were going to have at the cabin. I was excited about our trip, and it was really going to be the first vacation I'd ever taken as an adult.

As I turned my back to Nick to rinse the soap off my body, he started running his hands up and down my hips, moving them up and down while trailing kisses along the back of my neck and the top of my back. I moaned and pushed my ass in his direction, his hard-on poking me.

"Wow, I had no clue that the thought of going camping excited you so much," I joked, giggling a bit.

Once I was thoroughly washed off, I turned the water off and jumped out of the shower, leaving Nick and his erection standing inside.

"Nope, that's not happening. Not yet," I continued to joke, refusing him of the sex he was after.

"Oh come on," Nick said, jumping out of the shower behind me. I could hear the lust in his voice and see the desire in his eyes.

"Let's save until we get there. It will be more exciting," I announced, laughing and running into the bedroom.

I could hear Nick sighing, but he didn't follow me. I turned around just in time to see him looking down at his throbbing hard-on and shrugging to himself.

Less than an hour later, we were on the road. About an hour into the drive, we lost the signal of the radio station we were listening to so I started scanning the channels, trying to find something good.

Nick reached over and pulled me to him, wrapping

his arm around me and holding me close to his body. That was one thing I loved about his truck.

It has one long seat in the front instead of two individual seats. This allowed me to sit right next to him. It also gave me more than enough room to lie down if the mood struck me.

As we drove further out of the city and deeper into the country, I was in awe of our surroundings. There were trees as far as the eye could see and the sun had just started setting in the sky, casting deep purple shadows in the clouds. I'd never seen a view so breathtaking.

I placed my hand on his chest, rubbing it up and down as he drove. I loved how his muscles felt over the top of his shirt. I'd never been with somebody like him before. He was such a man, so powerful.

He was almost more of a beast than a man. That was a pretty fun way to describe him, but it was true. He was very much beast-like. He was a big, strong guy with a raw sexuality that drove me crazy every time he touched me. I loved it, and I loved him.

The longer we drove, the more I started to realize that we hadn't seen another driver in ages. We were driving away from civilization and towards our cabin, which was literally in the middle of nowhere.

We'd have all the privacy we wanted. Since there

wasn't anyone else out on the roads, I figured it would be a good time to give him a little surprise.

I reached over and started messing with the strap of his belt, trying to get it loosened without him knowing what I was doing.

I wasn't nearly as slick as I thought I was because he looked down just as I had the belt out of the buckle and was unbuttoning his pants. His erection popped out at me as soon as I had his zipper time.

"Wow, that didn't take any time at all," I said, looking up at him with a raised eyebrow.

"What can I say? You just have an effect on me," he responded while shifting his body behind the wheel so he could tug his pants down for me.

I grabbed his dick in my hand, causing him to sharply exhale before taking a deep breath in. I started to stroke him, slowly moving my hand up and down on him. Nick's eyes drifted away from the road and down towards me.

"Eyes on the road, mister," I told him as I leaned into him, kissing his neck and nibbling on his earlobes.

I lowered my head down and started kissing all over the head of his cock. It must have had an effect on him because the hairs on his legs were standing straight up.

Nick moaned as I opened my mouth and took his dick all the way into the back of my throat. He always complimented me on how well I could give head. I guess I was blessed with the lack of a gag reflex.

My hand tugged on while I ran my tongue all over his head. He grabbed a handful of my hair as I took him in and out of my mouth. Nick used my hair to push me even further down onto him. I always knew he was getting close when he started to control how fast my movements were.

I picked up the pace, knowing he was getting close. I moaned as I sucked, letting him know that going down on him was turning me on just as much as him. I loved pleasing my man.

As I sucked faster and faster, Nick started moving his hips around. Before I knew it, I felt his hot load hit the back of my throat before I swallowed it down.

"Fuck," Nick said. "I love you so fucking much."

I looked up at him and smiled.

"I love you too, Nick," I said with a smile before scooting in close to him, where I would remain for the rest of the trip.

13
NICK

Our trip to the cabin had been fantastic. We spent most of our time in bed. The rest of the time was filled with relaxing in the hot tub, hiking the trails that surrounded us and watching the sun rise and set.

It was beautiful out there. It reminded me of something you'd see on a postcard or in a painting.

Alexa decided that since we were going to be spending quite a bit of time at the cabin that summer, she was going to start a nature collection of things she found there. She found all kinds of neat things like different rocks and things of that nature.

Before we could blink, our week was over, and it was time to come back home to the real world. We had a blast with one another but the time had gone by too quickly. I was already looking ahead to the following month when we'd get to have the adventure all over again.

The night we got back, Alexa came to my apartment, something I'd gone out of my way to avoid.

"Oh no, no, no," she said. "This just isn't going to work."

"I know it's not the best babe, but it works. It's not like I spend a lot of time here."

"That's not what I mean. This apartment actually has a lot of potential, but I get the feeling you aren't the best when it comes to interior decorating."

"What are you trying to say?" I joked.

"You know exactly what I mean. I think this place could look really nice. It just needs a woman's touch."

"Yeah? Well, you can do whatever you want with is just as long as I don't come home to pink walls. At least leave a hint of a man living here."

"Okay, deal."

She didn't have to go back to work for a couple of days, so the plan was for her to crash at my place for the night. When I went to work the next morning, she'd stay there and take care of whatever decorating she wanted to do.

The workday was long. All I could think about all day was getting back to my apartment to see Alexa and find out what she'd done to my place.

On my way home, I decided to drop by the store to pick up some flowers for her. It would be my way of thanking her for helping me get my place in order.

I called Alexa's cell phone while I was in my car to find out if she was making something for dinner or if I needed to pick up something for us to eat while I was out. It rang four times and went to voicemail.

I waited a few minutes and tried again, only to be met with the same result. I tried again a third time and still got no answer. I found it odd that her phone would be going to voice mail.

She always answered my calls, no matter where she was or what she was doing.

Although it was odd that she wasn't answering her phone, I was sure there was a reasonable explanation for it. When I pulled into the parking lot for my apartment building, I saw her car parked in the lot, right where it had been that morning. I was glad she was there and figured she was either taking or a shower or napping.

I made my way into the building and walked down the hall. My door was unlocked, so I entered quietly, not wanting to disturb her if she was resting.

After shutting the door behind me, I turned to see her sitting at the kitchen table. She was seated with her back to me with her face looking down towards the floor.

"Honey, I'm home," I yelled jokingly as I kicked off

my shoes and went over to join her at the table. "These are for you," I said, holding the flowers out to her.

Alexa didn't move a muscle. She didn't say anything to me, and she didn't acknowledge the flowers I was holding in my hand. Instead, she kept looking at the table, her arms crossed in front of her.

"Babe? Is everything okay?" I asked after looking at her for a moment. Again, she didn't reply. She appeared to be frozen in time.

I was starting to get worried that something might be wrong with her, so I sat the flowers down on the table and went down to one knee next to her.

I reached out and touched her shoulder, prompting her to jump up from the table, jerking away from my touch.

"Shit," I yelled out complete involuntarily. I wasn't expecting the sudden movement, and she startled me.

I stood up, studying her face, completely confused by what was happening. Finally getting a good look, I saw that her eye makeup was smeared, and her eyes appeared to be puffy and bloodshot. It looked as though she'd been crying. When I touched her, her face contorted in fear and anger.

What in the world is happening here?

Alexa looked like she was in the middle of a panic

attack. I'd seen many people have them, but I'd never known her to have a problem with them.

Her breathing was deep and choppy, almost like she was trying to catch her breath after running. I didn't know what it was, but something was freaking her out. Something had her scared.

At that point, I noticed she was shaking. I also saw that she had some kind of paper in her hand. I tried to figure out what it was, but she had it gripped so tightly, it was crinkling in her fist.

"Alexa? You gotta talk to me. What the hell is happening? What's wrong with you?" I asked her, taking a step in her direction.

"Don't come near me," she shouted, taking a step away from me. "You just stay there and don't come any closer to me."

I didn't want to freak her out any more than she already was so I stopped dead in my tracks and looked at her, holding my hands up slightly as if to let her know that I wasn't going to move.

"What's the matter?" I asked softly. "What is it that you have there?"

"What this? You wanna know what this paper is?" she asked, holding it up in front of my face. "These are just your parole papers," she spat out with disgusted venom.

Her head started to shake, and her eyes began to fill

up with tears. It took me a minute to realize what she'd just said to me. I felt like I was in shock.

I felt like there was a huge weight suddenly on my chest, pushing down on me and making it hard to breathe. It felt so heavy that I felt like I could fall over.

That was when the reality of the situation truly hit me.

My stomach started tying itself in knots, and my heart physically began to ache.

No, this can't be happening. Not like this.

I didn't know what to do so I just stood there looking at her, studying her face with my mouth hanging open in shock. I didn't have a clue what I was supposed to say to her.

It wasn't something I'd gone through in my mind. I never wanted her to find out like this. Hell, I never intended for her to find out at all. I didn't have a plan for this situation.

There was nothing I could do to divert her hurt or anger. There were no lies I could tell that was going to fix it. I was fucked.

Alexa stood there in my kitchen, staring a hole right through me. Tears were streaming down her face, and she didn't even make an attempt to hide the fact she was crying.

I felt crushed, wanting nothing more than to hold her

and comfort her. I wished I could tell her that it was all a misunderstanding, that the paper she was holding was some kind of a mix-up, but I knew I couldn't do that because there was no mix-up.

There was no misunderstanding. We were at a stalemate, with me staring at her and her staring right back.

"So you were in prison?" Alexa finally asked, mercifully breaking the silence in the room. Her ordinarily sweet voice was nowhere to be found. It was instead replaced with the sound of disgust.

"Yes," I murmured as I exhaled and closed my eyes, not being able to handle the look on her face."

"What did you do, Nick? What did you do to get sent to prison? This wasn't even jail. You were in the penitentiary. You gotta do some fucked up shit to get put in the pen."

I didn't reply.

"Maybe I shouldn't even be asking you this," she continued. "I mean, you didn't tell me in the first place so I'm sure you'd just feed me some line of bullshit, wouldn't you? And what about your family, Nick? You've told me so many different things that none of them are adding up anymore. Was any of that the truth?" she added, putting things together right there in front of me.

I should have known that she would have figured it all

out eventually. She's a brilliant woman. She's always been a lot smarter than me.

She was college educated, and I didn't even finish high school. I'd known from the start that she was too good for me, but I held on because I loved her so much. I should have seen all of this coming. It was inevitable.

"Nick, answer me! You at least owe me that much," she yelled, snapping me out of my thoughts.

Her words had so much anger in them. They were filled with hate and loathing. I'd never seen her act like that before.

"Yes, Alexa. Yes, I was in prison, but it was for something idiotic. It was just a fight."

"Just a fight? I've known lots of guys who have gotten into fights. None of them were ever sent to prison for fighting. I call bullshit on that one. Try again."

"It was a fight. It was a fight that ended up very badly. The guy I was fighting hit his head and was in terrible shape for a while. I was brought up on attempted murder charges."

"Attempted murder?" she gasped, her face suddenly going flush. "I've been with someone who was convicted of attempted murder? Holy shit."

"It's not like that, Alexa. It's not like that at all. I didn't go looking for a fight. The other guy did. I didn't go out trying to murder someone. I'm sorry I didn't tell you before. I couldn't bring myself to tell you about it. I love you, and I didn't want to lose you over a stupid mistake.

"Uh-huh. And what about your family? What about everything you told me about them?"

"I don't have a family," I said coldly, looking across the room past her. I knew she was gone. I knew I had already lost the woman I loved.

"So let me get this straight. You lied about where you were before you moved here. Apparently, you've always lived here. You were just in prison. In fucking prison, Nick! Then you lied about your family. Has there been anything real about you? Have you told me anything in our entire relationship that wasn't complete and utter bullshit?"

I watched her as tears streamed quickly down her cheeks. Her face was contorted in pain. I could actually feel what she was feeling, and it was heartbreaking.

"I love you. That part has never been a lie," I told her.

I knew that those words weren't going to do any good, but I wanted to say them anyway. I wanted her to know that no matter how badly I screwed up, my love for her was the one thing that was always real.

Alexa laughed a short, involuntary laugh. It was as though she couldn't believe what I was saying. Her lips sneered in disgust and anger.

It was a side of her I'd never seen before. She shook

her head and started to say something, but she stopped herself. Instead, she tossed the parole papers onto the table in front of me, looked at me with pain in her eyes, and grabbed her purse on the way towards the door.

I didn't know what I was supposed to do. I was frozen in shock of what had just gone done. I couldn't say or do anything. The only thing I could do was stand in the kitchen and watch her walk out of my life forever.

She was opening my front door when I knew I had to stop her. I couldn't lose her. Not like that. Not without at least doing everything I could to convince her that I'm not that man anymore.

I run up behind her, close the door in front of her before she had a chance to leave. She jumped at my unexpected arrival. She may have even been a little frightened, but my intention wasn't to scare her.

I would never do her any harm. Even though I'd hurt her emotionally, there was no way I'd ever hurt her physically.

I'd hoped that she'd turn around to talk to me. At the very least, I just wanted her to hear me out. Instead, she remained facing the door, her hand firmly gripping the knob.

"I want to leave, Nick," she mumbled. I hated the shakiness that she had in her voice. She was scared of me. That was the last thing I wanted.

"Alexa, please don't do this," I begged of her with my hand still pressed against the door, preventing her from opening it until I at least tried to talk to her. "I love you more than anything in the world, Alexa. I've been waiting my entire life for you. I don't want to lose you. I can't lose you. Please don't walk out on me."

There was so much pressure building within my chest. I had a fear and panic in me that I never knew existed. I could feel tears welling up in my eyes and fought them off the best I could.

I'd always been told that crying was a form of weakness, so I never did it. I certainly didn't want to cry in front of her, but the tears were coming, and I didn't know if I had it in me to choke them back.

"Nick, please just let me go. I don't want to be here right now," she begged

I hated the way she was pleading with me. The shakiness in her voice increased with each word she said. I didn't want her to be afraid of me.

I didn't want to scare her any worse than I already had. I wasn't sure what to do. I didn't want her to go. I was afraid that if she left, I'd never see her again. At the same time, I didn't want to ruin any chance I had left, no matter how slim that chance was.

I certainly didn't want to make things any worse than they already were. I removed my hand from the door and took a few steps back. She threw it open and ran out. Just like that, Alexa was gone.

I didn't have much in life. Alexa was the only thing in my life that meant anything to me at all. She was my life. She was my entire existence.

Now, she was gone. I'd lost her, and there wasn't anything I was going to be able to do about it. There would be no talking my way out of it. I fucked up, and I was going to have to live with that reality.

A hollow, empty feeling filled my open as I closed the door before leaning against it and sliding down to the floor. I sat there, looking at my empty apartment and started to cry.

It was a new experience for me and one that I didn't like at all. I never cried when the state came and took me from foster family to foster family. I never cried when these families, who were supposed to love and care for me, beat me belts or choked me when I didn't act exactly how they wanted me to.

I didn't cry when I was convicted of attempted murder. I couldn't even remember the last time I cried.

That night was miserable to me. My mind wouldn't shut off, and there was no way I was going to be getting any sleep.

All I could think about were what-if scenarios that I couldn't do anything about. I thought about the things I should have done differently from day one. I thought about all the things I should have told her.

When I couldn't think about what I should have done differently. My mind turned to Alexa in general. I thought about how I felt the first time I laid eyes on her. I thought about the first time she and I had sex.

I thought about the week at the cabin that we'd just come back from. I thought about the way her body looked, the way she always smelled so good. I could still remember just the way she tasted. I sat in my apartment by myself for hours playing back all the time we spent together.

I spent most of the night remembering everything about her. I remembered the way she felt when we made love and the way I felt the first time I heard her tell me she loved me.

I couldn't go down with a fight. I couldn't let things end like that. She was mine. I knew I was right for her, whether or not she believed it at the moment.

As good as I was for her, I knew she was even better for me. I didn't just want Alexa, I needed her. I needed her in my life to keep me grounded. She kept me sane. I felt like she gave me a purpose to go on when everything else seemed impossible. In some ways, she was my reason for breathing.

Since I met her, she was the reason I got out of bed

every morning because I knew she'd be waiting for me at the end of the day. She was the kind of person that you only meet once in a lifetime. I couldn't let her go. I refused to let her go. I was willing to do whatever it was I needed to do.

I was going to get her back.

14

ALEXA

It had taken me a lot longer to get home than it usually did. It was hard to drive with shaking hands and the tears filling my eyes.

I was still having a hard time processing everything that had happened. It caught me off guard, and I was finding it especially difficult to wrap my head around it.

As I pulled into my parking lot, the tears had finally stopped, but my head continued to spin.

A million thoughts ran through my mind. Was any of this actually happening? Was it all a bad dream? Was I going to wake up relieved that none of it actually happened? As lovely as that would have been, I knew better. My world was being turned upside down.

How could Nick hide something like that from me?

He seemed so real. He seemed so trustworthy. He seemed so genuine.

When he told me he loved me, I was dumb enough to believe him. Instead, he made me out to look like a fool. I should have been used to that. He sure as hell wasn't the first person to do that to me.

There I was, being the naive, trusting girl that I always was. I was a fool who was willing to give myself completely to someone who didn't deserve it. I gave him the best of me, and all he did was lie to me and manipulate me so he could get what he wanted.

He told me what I wanted to hear so he could get into my panties and I let him. He used me for his own benefit. I thought he was different but in reality, he was just like any of the other assholes that I'd been with in the past.

I went inside my apartment and didn't even bother to take a shower. All I wanted to do was go to bed and put an end to the horrible day I'd just had.

I didn't even bother to take off anything other than my shoes. I crawled into bed, buried my face into my pillows and closed my eyes.

I intended to sleep until morning, but that ended up being much more complicated than I'd expected. Instead of resting up, I laid there, replaying the day's events.

The day was going fine. I was going through his apartment and organizing it for him. Early in the afternoon, I noticed the mailman out the window and figured I'd grab his mail for him so he wouldn't have to do it later.

I didn't figure he'd have a problem with it. He left the key sitting on the kitchen counter and as far as I knew, we didn't have any secrets to keep from one another.

I never even intended to go through his mail. I had just placed it down on the counter when a return address caught my eye.

It was from the Minnesota Department of Corrections.

I knew that meant it was from a jail or prison in the state and figured it was probably put into the wrong mailbox. I was looking to see who it was addressed to so I could get it to the right person when I saw that it was actually sent to Nick.

I spent the next few minutes being very conflicted.

Why would Nick be getting something from the Minnesota Department of Corrections?

It didn't make any sense. I made the decision to open it. It wasn't a decision that I'm particularly proud of, but I made it, and there was no turning back. I had to know what it was.

Why would it matter anyway? If Nick didn't have anything to hide, me opening it would have been no big deal. Instead of the letter being something harmless, it was a letter from his parole officer, letting him know when and where Nick needed to come in and meet with him.

My mind spun, and I was in shock. I felt like I had tunnel vision as I stared at the paper, not being able to see anything but the white sheet in front of me.

Had Nick been in prison without bothering to tell me? The letter referred to the Ramsey County Correctional Facility, which was about an hour from where we lived.

How was it possible that he could have been at the Ramsey County Prison in Minnesota? Nick and Curtis had both said that he'd lived in California before coming to work at the construction company Curtis owned. Surely he would have mentioned being in prison, wouldn't he? Everything was starting to sink in as I sat in his kitchen.

Nick had never been in California.

That was just a big line of bullshit that he fed to me. He lied to my face. All of the things that he'd told me he'd done had all been lies. Everything he said about his life had been lies.

All of the stories about his childhood and his family, none of them made sense. None of them seemed to add up over time. Even something as simple as what he used to call grandma changed with the stories. Sometimes he would refer to her as Granny and other times he called her maw-maw.

It was odd that he didn't have a specific thing he called her all the time. I remember thinking it was weird before but it never seemed like something that was worth questioning him about.

One thing I did notice was that when Nick would tell me about his past, specifically anything about his family, he never showed any emotion whatsoever.

He wasn't happy or sad when he told me about them. The stories were just empty. It was different when he told me stories about Curtis.

The two of them obviously had a solid bond. They each thought of the other as their brother. That was evident from the way they both spoke of one another, but none of that emotion was ever present when he talked about family.

I wondered if any of the things he told me about his family were true at all.

I have no clue how long I sat at his kitchen table, waiting for him to come home. I just remember sitting there, wondering what was going to happen when he got there.

I didn't know if I should leave before he got there, especially since I didn't know what he'd gone to prison for.

Would I be in danger if I stayed there? Was Nick a dangerous man? Was he a violent offender of some sort? Did he kill someone? Did he do something to a woman he was dating?

He had never done anything to me in the time we'd been together. Hell, he had never cursed at me or even so much as yelled at me. For our entire relationship, he always treated me so well. He always acted like a total gentleman. He was a sweetheart.

How much of that was an act, though?

Maybe the way he was treating me was all a cover-up. Perhaps it was to hide the person he really was. I was so deep in thought, I didn't even hear my cell phone ringing over and over.

The true panic didn't set in, however, until Nick walked into his apartment. I'd lost all track of time and didn't realize that it was already time for him to be home.

He appeared in front of me before I'd had a chance to decide how I wanted to handle the situation. I was still trying to wrap my head around everything when he appeared next to me, touching my shoulder. That touch was more than I could handle. That was when I lost it.

I couldn't put up with a man who had lied to me every day. I couldn't endure the betrayal and the deceit. When I walked out the door, I had already made the decision that I was never going to see him again.

I didn't care that he had a bunch of his things at my apartment. I didn't want to think about that. I could get his things back to him somehow.

At the moment, however, I needed to get in contact with Kim and Curtis because Nick hadn't been the only person who was being dishonest.

15

NICK

I didn't understand where she could be. I'd been sitting at Alexa's kitchen table for at least two hours, waiting for her to come but she hadn't arrived. She should have been home long before.

She probably wouldn't have let me come by if I had called and asked, so I just dropped in, using the key she had given me to let myself into the apartment.

I needed to talk to her, and she was ignoring all of my calls and text messages. I hated doing things the way I was going about doing them, but it was the only way that would work.

I received a call earlier that afternoon from Curtis, telling me that Alexa had been at his house, and she was pissed.

She insisted that Kim and Curtis explain to her why

they didn't tell her about me. Fortunately, Kim wasn't home at the time, and Curtis was able to talk to Alexa in private.

She was pissed off that Curtis didn't tell her about me, but he explained that I was his best friend and needed his help. After much begging and pleading, Alexa agreed not to tell Kim about it. Whether or not she would keep true to that agreement remained to be seen.

During their conversation, Alexa told him exactly what she was feeling towards me. She said that she felt like I did nothing but manipulate her. Hearing him say that hurt my heart unbelievably bad.

I didn't want her to think that way as it was never my intention. I never wanted to hurt her. She didn't know what I was feeling towards her. She was wrong about my feelings and my intentions.

All along, my intentions were good. I just needed to find some way to get my point across to her. I needed her to see that I was sincere. I needed to be able to prove these things to her.

As it got dark outside, the inside of the apartment darkened as well. I didn't bother turning on a light, so I sat in the darkness waiting for her. Besides, if she came home and saw a light on inside, she might not come in, and I really needed to be able to talk to her.

I don't know how long I sat there in the dark before I

finally heard her key unlocking her door. I tried to stay relaxed, but my nerves were getting the best of me. I'd practiced what I was going to say to her over and over again in my head for the previous few hours, but all those thoughts disappeared. All of those thoughts were replaced by a blank space.

My legs were shaking as I stood up from the chair and waited for her to turn on the lights. She always came in, turned on the lights and did something in the kitchen. That night was different than what I was used to. Instead of flipping the lights on, I heard her footsteps walk through the living room and into her bedroom. The first light she turned on was a small lamp that sat on one of her end tables.

Slowly, I started making my way into her bedroom. The whole conversation would have been much easier if she had walked in to see me sitting at her table. Now that she was in her room, the fact that I was there might scare. I didn't want her to be afraid of me. I didn't want her to look at me and see fear, hurt, and disgust in her eyes.

If I had it my way, I would have just remained in the shadows until she came around, but I knew that wasn't going to happen unless I had a chance to talk to her. While I tried to figure out how to announce my presence, I stood in the hallway, watching as she sat down on her bed.

I'd never seen a woman look so broken before, and I felt horrible knowing that I was the reason.

I wanted so badly to be able to walk into her bedroom, tell her everything was going to be okay and have her actually believe me.

I wanted to hold her and make her feel safe. I wanted to do whatever I could do to make her forget all the things I screwed up. I wanted to somehow make her forget that everything had happened. I wanted to hear her telling me that she loved me again.

Unfortunately, none of that was going to happen, so I stayed in the hallway until I figured out a better plan.

Alexa was sitting on the edge of her bed with her face buried in her hands. She started to shake, which was when I realized she was crying. I hated seeing her like that.

My insides were torn up with guilt from putting her in that position. I hated seeing her like that, so I stepped into her room.

"Alexa?" I muttered, not wanting to alarm her.

She let out a yelp and jumped up off her bed, surprised that she wasn't alone in the apartment. She stood there staring at me without saying a word for what felt like hours. I tried to get a read on her expression, but she had her poker face on.

"I want you to leave, Nick," she finally said, her voice

sounding frail and weak. She was no longer crying, but there was no hiding the fact that she had been. I felt uncomfortable standing in her doorway, but I really needed her to listen to me. I took a couple of steps towards her, but she backed off, her body tensing up.

"I mean it, Nick! I want you out of my apartment right now!" she demanded, this time with more bass in her voice.

"Alexa, please hear me out. Please give me a chance to explain everything to you," I begged. My mouth was suddenly parched, causing my voice to crack.

"No. You had your chance to explain everything to me since the day you met me. Now it's too late. I don't want to hear any of your excuses. I can't listen to any of it," she said as she fought back the tears. She wouldn't even look me in the eyes.

"Alexa, please, at least give me a chance. I love you. I'm not the person you think I am."

"Yeah, I think I've already figured that out."

"That's not what I mean, Alexa. I talked to Curtis, and he told me that you were over to see him. I know you think that I'm a liar and that I took advantage of you, but that isn't true at all. I mean, yeah, I wasn't honest with you about my past. I didn't want to tell you that I did time in prison. I knew there was no way in hell you would have ever given me the time of day if I would have told you that. I mean, look at you. You wouldn't have ever given me a chance. Am I right?"

I waited for an answer of some sort, but she continued looking straight down at her floor.

"I needed to be someone else, somebody much better than the man I had become," I continued. "I was already starting my life over, and I needed a clean slate. I knew I wanted you from the first night we met, and I knew that in order to have any chance at all with you, I'd have to show you that I was good enough. I had to show you that I was worth taking a chance on. The only way I could do that was to act like I had a healthy upbringing. I couldn't let you know how fucking broken I really am so I acted like I had a normal past with a normal family. I was stupid to think it would work. It was really fucking stupid. You have no idea how many times I wanted to tell you the truth about who I was and the things I'd done but I couldn't. By that time, it had all snowballed out of control, and I had no way out."

For the first time, Alexa looked up and was actually making eye contact with me as I talked.

"I never wanted to lie to you, Alexa. I didn't want to deceive you. If I could go back and fix it, I would, even if it meant you and I never would have been together. I wanted to tell you everything, and I think I would have whenever the time was right. It was dumb to believe that you'd never find out about any of my issues. I'm really sorry.

I mean, I fell in love with you the first night I met you. I hate the fact that you're hurting because of me. I never wanted you to hurt. I never wanted any of this. The only thing I wanted from the beginning was you. That's still all I want."

I took a couple steps toward her and this time, she didn't back away. I was standing directly in front of her, looking down at her tiny frame, which seemed even more fragile than it usually did.

She looked up at me but had a blank look in her eyes. She didn't say anything. I reached out and touched her cheek, which prompted her to pull away, walking around to the other side of her bed.

"How dare you? After what you've put me through, how dare you come over here and try to touch me. Don't you dare touch me," she began to scream. "I want you to turn around and leave. I want you out of my apartment this instant. I want you out of here, and I want you to leave my key on the way out."

"Alright, I can see that you're not ready to talk about any of this just yet, and that's fine. We don't have to talk about anything right now. You're going to need a little bit of time and space. I can respect that. I'll give you a few days or so to think, and then I'll come back by and see if you're ready to talk then," I said, being entirely sincere.

I flashed a slight smile at her before turning to walk out of her room and towards the front door.

"Nick!" she yelled right as I was about to leave. "I mean it. I want you to leave the key to the apartment before you go.

"No," I told her after standing there complimenting her request.

"No? What do you mean no? You can't say no."

"I just mean no, Alexa," I responded before walking out the door and going to my truck.

16

NICK

I let a few days go by before I even thought about trying to make contact with Alexa again. It killed me to walk out of her apartment earlier in the week, but it had killed me even more to not be able to see her or talk to her since. Whenever my cell phone would ring, I would hold my breath, hoping it was her calling.

Unfortunately, it never was.

Since Alexa and I got together, we had spent very few days apart from one another. Even when we weren't together, we'd talk on the phone or send text messages back and forth.

For the first few nights, after we split, I felt like I was in shock. Eventually, that feeling wore off and was replaced with emptiness. I felt like I was lost. All I could do was go to work before coming back to my apartment to pace back and forth on the floor.

I couldn't force myself to eat. I barely got any sleep. It had been too long, and I couldn't take it anymore. That Saturday, I decided that I needed to see her and at least try to talk to her again. I knew she had a day off coming up, so I waited until that day and drove over to her apartment.

Her SUV wasn't there, and I didn't want to go inside uninvited like I did last time. That might cause even more tension, and that definitely wasn't needed. Instead, I parked my truck and waited for her to come home.

I was waiting in my truck for close to two hours before I spotted her pulling into the parking lot. As she got out of her SUV, she looked right over in my direction. She was completely aware that I was there.

I figured the fact that she saw that I was waiting for her would be a good thing. Hopefully, she'd know that I really meant what I'd said to her.

She'd see that I was genuinely sorry and realize how desperate I was to have her back in my life. She'd know that I meant it when I told her I loved her. If only things could have been that easy.

Alexa completely ignored the fact that I was there and proceeded to grab the things she had in her vehicle. It looked like she'd been to the grocery store and a couple of department stores.

The back of her SUV was filled with bags. Once she grabbed as much as she could, she made her way towards the door. I figured that was the perfect time for me to make my move, so I jumped out of my truck, grabbed the rest of the bags and made my way to her door just as she was coming back out.

If looks could kill, I would have been dead on her front porch.

"Nick, you need to put the bags down and go back to your truck. I don't need your help, and you're not coming inside," she said, standing in front of the door with her arms crossed in front of her.

"Well, I'm not going to put any of these bags down unless it's inside so it looks like we might have ourselves a little stalemate here," I responded, smiling at her with a crooked smirk.

I wasn't trying to be a smart-ass, even though I was coming across that way. I was just trying to keep to situation light to keep her from feeling on edge. Alexa stood there staring at me, dumbfounded by how hard-headed I could be. Finally, she shook her head and walked back into her apartment.

I followed Alexa inside and sat her bags in the kitchen. She had already busied herself with putting her groceries away and was doing everything she could to avoid even looking in my direction.

I stood there for a minute, hoping she would eventually say something to me. When she didn't, I started helping her by taking some of the things out of her bags for her, keeping my eyes on her the entire time. Eventually, she slammed the refrigerator door as hard as she could and turned to face me.

I was expecting to see her face twisted in anger, but instead, I saw tears running down her cheeks.

"Nick, can you please just stop this?" she pleaded.

"Alexa," I started as I walked over to the fridge, standing directly in front of her.

"Please, Nick," she interrupted. "I want you to stop this. I don't know how much more of this I can take. Can't you see how much you've hurt me? Can't you see how much you're hurting me now? Do you even care?"

"Yes, I care. What kind of question is that? Would I be here if I didn't care? Do you think I want to hurt you? Hurting you is the last thing I ever wanted to do. I love you more than you could ever know. I love you so much. I just want to do whatever I can to fix this. I want to make this right."

"How do you expect to fix this? This isn't something that can be fixed. You fix things that are broken. This relationship isn't broken. It's far beyond that. It's been destroyed. There's nothing that can be done about that. What part of this are you not understanding? You lied to me about where you've been. You said you were from California when you were actually sitting in a prison cell. I can't handle that. I don't want to be in a relationship with you. I don't love you at all. I don't want to be with you. I don't want anything to do with you. The only thing I want is for you to walk out that door and never come back!"

Alexa was staring up at me, talking to me through a clenched jaw. I'd never seen that side of her, and it made me miss the fun and carefree girl that I'd come to love.

"Alexa, think about what you're saying to me. There's no way you can mean that" I replied, stepping in so close to her that her back was up against the fridge.

"Nick, you need to stop. Don't come any closer," she warned, putting her hand on my chest to keep some separation.

I wasn't giving up that easily. I grabbed the hand that was on my chest and moved it to my cheek. I hoped that if she touched me, something might come back to her.

She tried to pull her hand away, but I wouldn't let her. I knelt down just a little and pushed my hips into hers.

"Nick, let me go," she whispered.

Alexa was breathing heavily now. I wasn't sure if it was because she was scared of me, even though I was trying to be as non-threatening as possible, or if it was because she was turned on.

If it was the latter, I wanted to find out. She was wearing a dress, so I took my hand and ran it up on the inside of her leg. Her body moved with my touch.

"I wish you would understand, Alexa, that I love you so much, and it's impossible for me to just let you go that easily. Without you in my life, it feels like a part of me has died," I whispered into her ear as I started to rub at her panties with my fingers.

I thought she was enjoying it. I was waiting for her to turn and moan into my ear like she'd done so many times before. Instead, I heard her begin to sob.

What in the fuck was I thinking? How could I have actually thought that would have worked? I was trying to seduce her into taking me back and instead, I only made her more afraid of me than she already was. I knew I fucked things up even more so I let her go and stepped away from her. She cowered on the floor, looking horrified.

"I'm so sorry, Alexa. I didn't mean for any of that to happen," I told her, sincerely meaning it.

I wasn't sure what had come over me. The actions I was taking were all wrong. I felt like a monster. I shouldn't have even been there. I turned around and ran from the apartment.

17
NICK

I felt as though my soul was being tormented. I was being eaten up by guilt. How could I have been so stupid to have frightened her again?

All I wanted to do was talk to her and show her that I cared about her. How hard can something like that be?

Apparently, it's pretty fucking hard because I managed to screw it up yet again. I knew I'd ruined my chance and Alexa was never going to be mine again.

Not wanting to go home to my apartment to sit by myself, I drove around the streets of Minnesota with no particular destination in mind. I was just trying to get her off my mind.

Somehow, I ended up at the same seedy strip club Curtis had told me about not long after I was released. I wasn't interested in watching the girls dance.

Instead, I grabbed a seat at the bar and started downing shots. Typically, it would have taken me a ton of alcohol to get drunk, but I hadn't drunk since Alexa, and I had gotten together. She wasn't really into drinking all that much.

The alcohol was quickly doing its job, the buzz making my body feel numb. It wasn't enough, though.

It was my heart that I wanted to go numb.

I wanted to be able to not care at all. I wanted everything that I was thinking to disappear from my brain. I wanted to forget that Alexa ever existed or, at the very least, not care about her anymore. I wanted to forget about the way she felt when I held her in my arms. I wanted to forget how it felt when she touched me.

No matter how much I wanted to forget, it was impossible to do. Every time I closed my eyes, I could hear the sound of her laughter and see her face smiling at me.

I missed the way she and I could joke around. I wanted that back more than anything.

What was I supposed to do, though? She made it clear that she didn't want anything to do with me.

"Hey big guy, it's been a while," said a throaty voice standing behind me.

I turned slowly on my barstool to see who in the hell was talking to me. It was the girl that I'd hooked up with the last time I was in there.

I didn't invite her to join me, but she took a seat next to me anyway. She flashed a smile at me while casually grazing my arm with her fingers as she sat.

"Can I get another drink?" I yelled at the bartender.

"I think you've had enough. I'm cutting you off," he replied smugly.

I must have been slurring my words pretty severely at that point because, most of the time, people can't tell when I'm drunk.

I wanted to argue with him and tell him that I was okay but decided against it. Technically, I wasn't even supposed to be drinking and I sure as hell wasn't supposed to be in a strip club.

Both would have violated my parole and could have sent my ass back to prison. Instead, I pulled out my wallet and paid for my drinks.

"You leaving already?" the girl asked as I started making my way towards the door. "I was hoping you'd stick around a little longer. Maybe we could have a repeat of last time."

She stood up next to me, leaning into me with her hands slowly moving up my chest. The bartender looked over and rolled his eyes. When I looked down at her, all I could see was Alexa.

"We could have a little fun," I mumbled. "Why don't we go somewhere we can have a little privacy."

"Sure thing, sweetheart. You remember where the rooms are, right?"

"Yeah, I know where they are, but that's not where I want to go. I don't want to be here at all," I told her, walking out the door. She followed behind, stopping as soon as she got outside.

"I can't leave. I've gotta work tonight," she said.

"Look, honey, if it's money you want, I've got it," I said, pulling my wallet out of my back pocket and holding it up in front of her. "You should probably take me up on my offer."

The stripper stood in the parking lot, trying to figure out what she should do.

"Okay. Can you hang out for twenty minutes? I'll meet you back out here then."

"Fine but try to hurry."

I waited in my truck before she finally showed up carrying her things. I grabbed her hand while she was getting in, helping her in.

"So where are we headed?"

I didn't answer her. I just put my truck in gear and drove back to my place. I hated my apartment, but this girl was nothing more than a typical stripper. I wasn't trying to impress her.

I walked into the apartment, with her right behind me, her high heels clicking loudly with each step she took.

Inside my apartment, I went into my bedroom and opened the closet door. There were some things I wanted to grab before things went any further. I gathered what I needed and arranged them out onto the bed.

"So now that I'm here with you, how much are we talking?" the stripper asked.

"I'm paying you $300, and for that, you'll do what I ask."

"Three-hundred bucks? What do I have to do to earn that kind of money."

"You can start but shutting the fuck up and putting this stuff on," I told her, pointing to the bed.

She looked confused when she took a closer look. On the bed, I had sat out a red sweater and a bottle of perfume.

"So you're going to pay me $300 to wear some clothes and perfume? What's the catch man?" she asked as she pulled the sweater over the dress she was wearing, followed by a couple of squirts of the perfume.

"The catch is that you have to do things exactly as I tell you to. You got it?"

My voice was hard and cold as I was telling her what she had to do and I didn't even care. She looked at me like I was some sort of creep and, at the time, maybe that's what I was being. It didn't matter, though. This wasn't about her. It was all about me.

"So who do you want me to be tonight?" she asked as I sat down on the edge of the bed.

"Your name is Alexa, just like last time," I responded.

"Alright, sweetheart. If that's what you want, that's what you're going to get."

"Don't call me sweetheart. She isn't into shit like that. You have to talk like her. She only calls me Nick. None of that sweetheart or honey bullshit. Nick and nothing else."

"Fine Nick, that's what I'll call you."

"Your voice is too deep. She doesn't have all that bass in her voice. Her voice is higher and more feminine. Just make your voice higher and get over here."

I spent the next hour going over the rules and telling her all the things she needed to say and do. She protested a bit, telling me that she wasn't going to remember everything I was telling her to do.

If she wanted my money, she was going to do everything exactly as I told her.

"You know, this isn't going to be a one-time thing, right?" I asked, drawing a look of concern from her. "I want you to come over to my apartment every single night this week. As soon as you get off work, I want you over here. I want you here wearing this exact outfit and wearing this exact perfume. I want you to act the way she acted. I want you to talk the way she talked. I want you to be here."

"Don't you think this is a little weird, Nick?"

"No Alexa, I don't," I replied, oblivious to the fact that I was losing my mind. "You don't even have to knock when you get here. Just walk in and ask me about my day and tell me about yours. I don't want to hear about any of that stripper shit. I want to know how your day working at the gas station was. If you do these things, you'll get paid every time."

She nodded her head in agreement.

"Good. Now turn around," I said once I was done telling her everything she needed to know.

She did exactly as I asked without hesitation. She faced the wall while I stood up and turned off the lights, leaving nothing but the faint moonlight coming through the windows.

The lights being off allowed me to forget who I was actually in the room with, giving me a more authentic experience.

I crept up behind her and wrapped my arms around her waist. She didn't have the same curvy shape that Alexa had, but it would have to do. I rested my head on her shoulder, breathing in the smell of the perfume from her neck.

"Thank you, Alexa. Thank you so much for giving me one more chance."

"You don't have to thank me," she said as she made

her voice higher as I had requested. "I'm yours, Nick. I'm not going anywhere. I love you."

"I love you too, Alexa. I love you so much."

I pushed her hair to the side and began kissing her neck. It must have tickled because she laughed and tried pulling away from me. I wasn't going to let her go, though. Not this time. I held her right where I wanted her.

Before she could say another word, I reached up under her dress, grabbed her panties and pulled them down before plunging my fingers into her pussy. There was just one problem. She wasn't the slightest bit wet.

This wasn't right.

Alexa was always wet anytime I touched her. It seemed that just being in my presence was enough to have her ready to go. This bitch was bone dry.

She was ruining everything!

That was the moment I snapped out of it. What the hell was I thinking? There was nobody who was going to be able to take Alexa's place, especially not some second-rate stripper.

"You need to get out," I yelled, catching her by surprise.

"What? Get out? What do you mean get out?"

"I mean get out of my apartment. This was a mistake."

"How in the fuck am I supposed to get home?"

"Take the money. I don't want it. Just leave!"

I hurried her to the door, locking it behind her before I jumped into the shower. I felt like I had to cleanse myself of what I'd just done. It was stupid of me to think that my loneliness could be cured by creating some kind of clone of Alexa.

She was irreplaceable.

I needed the real thing. I needed my Alexa back. I needed to show her that I loved her and let her know that, no matter what, I was going to fight for her because she was worth it.

18

ALEXA

The summer was extremely long. I was going to be advancing to store manager by the end of the year, so I had a lot of things to keep me busy at work but the evenings weren't very much fun.

I wasn't hanging out with Kim and Curtis all that much anymore. It was weird to be over there and not say anything to Kim about Nick. She'd ask all the time, but I never wanted to talk about it. Eventually, I found it best to keep my distance.

Once the summer was coming to an end, and my work schedule was beginning to get back to normal, Nick started to pop up again. Nearly every afternoon when I returned home from work, Nick would be sitting on a bench between my apartment and the apartment next door.

There was no way to miss him.

I walked by him as I made my way to the door.

At first, his mere presence scared the shit out of me. I had no idea what he was truly capable of.

I didn't think he wanted to hurt me. He'd had plenty of chances to do that if that's what he wanted to do. Still, I watched plenty of crime shows on television, and that alone was enough to make me wonder whether or not I was safe.

For the first couple of weeks, I told him to leave me alone and to just go home. He would get up and leave, only to be sitting in the same place the next day. I threatened to call the cops and have a restraining order placed against him if he came back.

Even that didn't stop him.

Of course, I never called the police or applied for a restraining order. As upset as he had made me, I didn't want him to have any trouble with the law, especially because he was out on parole. I didn't want to be the reason he ended up back in prison.

Being too nice to people has always been one of my most significant problems, and there I was, being a lot nicer to Nick than I probably should have been. I couldn't help it, though. That's just the kind of person I am. It was true that when Nick lied to me, he'd hurt me badly.

There was a time when I never wanted to see him

again. I wanted absolutely nothing to do with him. Over time, however, I started to rethink things. I began to evaluate what my feelings were.

The thoughts that Nick had only gotten with me so he could use me and manipulate me were beginning to slowly fade away. I started coming to the realization that his feelings for me were real, even though he went about everything in the worst possible way. The only thing I wasn't sure about was what those true feelings were precisely.

Did he love me or was he obsessed with me?

I had no clue. The only thing I knew was that he told me he wasn't going to let me go without a fight, and he was proving that to me.

Nick told me every day that he loved me and begged for me to sit down and talk to him. He told me that all he wanted was to have me back in his life. I wasn't ready to talk to him. Not yet anyway.

Instead, I ignored him, walking into my apartment without even looking in his direction. I hoped that if I ignored him, it might make it easier for him to let me go.

Maybe he would realize that I'd meant what I said, and he'd be able to move on with his life. I didn't want him to spend every day outside of my apartment just to try to talk to me. I didn't want that for either one of us.

More importantly, however, I didn't want him to

realize how hard it was for me to walk right by him on a daily basis and not talk to him.

There was a giant pat of me that was still very much pissed off about the lies he'd told me. I was petrified that I'd been with an ex-convict and didn't have a clue. It wasn't like he was arrested for some kind of non-violent crime.

He'd been in prison for attempted murder.

That was one thing I never understood. I'd never so much as seen him lose his temper so how he ended up in a bar fight was beyond me.

I had a battle going on inside my heart. The part of me that was still mad at him was fighting with the part of me that still loved him. The fact that he was obviously such a hardened man but still let me in was not lost on me. It probably took him a lot to let his guard down, especially after what he'd been through.

I'm sure it was difficult for him to show any emotions, especially after the childhood he was brought up in. For someone who had been so broken to be able to love me so openly and genuinely was something truly unique. He treated me far better than any man had in the past.

The two of us also had an incredible sexual pull to one another. There had been many nights when I sat at home by myself and thoughts of our time together would creep into my mind.

I would remember lying there wrapped up in his strong arms, reminiscing about how safe and protected he always made me feel. When I was with him, I felt like there was nobody who could touch me.

Nobody would be able to hurt me. Never in a million years would I have thought that he'd be the person that would hurt me the most.

As summer ended, the season gave way to fall, my favorite time of the year. I loved watching the leaves on the trees turn into beautiful shades of autumn colors. I enjoyed the feeling of the brisk wind hitting me in the face while the sounds of the drying leaves crunching beneath my feet surrounded me. There was something calming about the season. I don't know what it was exactly, but it seemed to relax my soul.

I'd had to stay late after work one night and got home quite a bit later than usual. The temperature had dropped, and we were getting ready for our first significant snow of the year. Even though the temperature outside was barely above freezing, Nick was still sitting there when I got there.

"Hey," he said, smiling through teeth that looked like they were about to start chattering.

He had excitement in his eyes like he was happy to finally be seeing me for the day. I don't know what it was, but I shot him a smile.

"Hi Nick," I said in response.

Nick cocked his head and looked at me. He reminded me of an excited puppy who is trying to figure out what you're doing. He had a look of surprise on his face, not quite believing that I had spoken to him after ignoring him for so long.

"You need some help?" he asked, referring to the large number of bags I'd been carrying.

I wasn't sure what to do. I began fighting with myself in my head and questioning whether or not I was making a mistake in even speaking to him.

"Uh, yeah, sure," I told him. "I've got a few bags left in the car if you want to grab them for me."

19
NICK

I jumped up off the bench and ran to retrieve the rest of her bags. My heart was racing, and I felt as though I was in a bit of shock. I couldn't believe what was happening. I needed to calm myself down, though.

Her letting me help her carry some things in didn't mean anything. The last time I'd been inside her apartment, I'd also helped her carry bags and the day ended very badly for both of us.

I tried to push that experience out of my mind. I needed to focus on what was happening right then and there. She'd finally spoken to me. I was finally getting the opportunity that I'd waited too long for. I just had to be smart and make smart choices this time around.

Setting the bags on her kitchen table, I turned to look at her. She had her back to me, emptying the bags. It looked like she was getting ready for Halloween as she'd purchase decorations for her windows along with big bags of candy. I smiled watching her, remembering how much she loved every holiday, regardless of which one it was.

"So, here we are," Alexa said after putting the last of the things away.

She leaned back against the kitchen counter, forcing a smile across her lips. It was nice to see a smile on her face again, although it didn't look nearly as good as the smile she used to wear when we were happy together. I could tell she was nervous and uncomfortable. I hated the fact that she was so tense because of me.

"How in this hell did this happen, Alexa?" I blurted out, not bothering to think about what I was going to say before opening my mouth.

I was worried about what her response was going to be. Was she going to say all the things she'd said before? Was she going to remind me that everything happened because of me? Was she going to tell me that we split up because I was a manipulator and a lying asshole?

I braced myself to hear hurtful words, but they didn't come. Instead, she opened her mouth the say something but decided against it. She looked up at me with deep sadness buried within her eyes.

"I honestly have no idea, Nick," she finally said. "I honestly have no idea."

Alexa stood up straight, no longer leaning on the counter. All of a sudden she looked strong and confident, a very different look than she'd had just seconds before.

"I really don't know, but all of these things that you've been doing, showing up here every day, it all has to stop."

Alexa was looking me directly in the eyes as I was trying to hide the hurt in them. Once again, I was being rejected, and I didn't know if I was going to be able to handle it again. My stomach felt queasy as I listened to her continue.

"I know why you're doing all of this, Nick. I really do. You're doing this because you love me and you're trying to prove it to me, right?"

I nodded my head.

"That's the thing, Nick. I don't doubt that you love me. I know you do. But none of this is healthy for you. You need to stop doing this for you. It's not fair to you. It's not fair to me. It's just not good for anyone."

20
ALEXA

I was trying to make things as easy as I could on him. I wasn't trying to make him feel bad. I hated the effect my words were having on him. I could see in his face that he was being beaten down. He looked like a lost puppy. I tried to choose my words more carefully.

"Listen, Nick. There's been a lot of things that have happened between us, and I'm not trying to hurt you. Hurting you is the last thing I want to do. I just think you should forget about me and move on."

I didn't even realize that I'd been making my way towards him while I talked but before I knew it, I was standing directly in front of him, looking up into his sad eyes.

When he made eye contact with me, I was caught off

guard as the sudden desire for him built up within me. Why in the hell did he have to be so damn attractive?

"That's just not going to happen, Alexa," he told me.

His words were not threatening nor did he mean for them to be. He wasn't saying them to scare me or to attempt to force me into taking him back. They were simply facts. He wasn't going to give up.

This was a talk that we'd both been needing to have for a long time. I knew it was going to be hard to have the discussion, but I had no clue it was going to be that hard.

The big, strong guy I'd come to know looked like he was going to break down in tears at any moment. I felt like I should say something but I had no idea what words would be helpful in that situation. Instead, I closed my eyes and took a deep breath.

With my eyes closed, I felt Nick touching my cheek. It was a soft, gentle touch. The kind of touch that always surprised me. You wouldn't expect someone so big to be able to touch you so softly. I liked it. It was a touch that I missed on a daily basis.

Still, I should have recoiled and pulled away from that touch. It wasn't fair to him for me to say one thing and then act in a different manner. I didn't want to lead him on. I didn't want to confuse him as to what was happening.

Hell, I didn't want to confuse myself.

As much as I wanted to pull away from his touch, I couldn't make myself do it. It was almost like he'd put a spell on me. Before I knew what hit me, he leaned in and gave me a soft kiss on the lips.

This wasn't one of the typical aggressive kisses that we'd shared a hundred times. This kiss was almost too gentle for a man like him to be able to give. Even though our lips barely grazed each other, I could feel the electricity shooting through my body.

He kissed me again, this time a little harder. I could feel my insides tossing and turning, and my pussy felt like it was on fire. Nick kissed me a third time, now slipping his tongue into my mouth while cradling my face in his hands.

I was running my hands up and down his chest, feeling his muscles flex as he moved. I kissed him back. I wanted him so bad. I wanted to rip his clothes off and have him take me right there on the kitchen table.

Right as I was about to grab the bottom of his shirt in an attempt to pull it off his body, he let go of my face and stepped away from me. He took a deep breath before a smile spread across his face. He appeared to be a different person. He wasn't the same broken man I'd seen for so long.

"Thank you, Alexa," he said.

"What are you thanking me for?" I asked, entirely unsure of what was happening.

He just smiled even bigger and thanked me again before stepping back towards me and placing his hands on my shoulder.

"You have no idea how badly I've needed this," he said.

I didn't know what to say to him, but I knew I'd done exactly what I was trying to avoid. I told him one thing and acted in an entirely different manner. Now I'd put all these thoughts and feelings in Nick's head, and I didn't want to do that.

"What's the matter?" Nick said, realizing that I was conflicted.

"We really shouldn't have done that. That was a bad idea. I shouldn't have let that happen," I told him as I buried my face in my hands.

I felt like the walls were closing in on me and I needed to put some space between the two of us. I walked out of the kitchen and into the living room. Nick, of course, followed right behind me.

"Alexa, it's okay. I realize that you may still need some more time. I'm fine with that. I can give you all the time you need," he told me, a smile forming on his face once again. "I can see that you still love me, and that's all I've wanted to know this entire time. If you're not ready yet, that's fine. I've waited this long, and I can wait longer."

He leaned in and told me he loved me in my ear before giving me a light kiss on the cheek.

After that, he didn't say another word. He just smiled at me one more time before turning and walking out of the apartment. I stood in place for what felt like forever.

What did I just do?

21

NICK

Even though Alexa had told me that she shouldn't have let me kiss her, I was in a better mood than I'd been in for a long time. Although I had been there, it all felt like a dream, and I was having trouble processing the fact that things had gone down the way they did.

After months of being apart and her not even willing to speak to me, I was finally able to touch her once again. I was able to kiss her and feel her breath on me. I was pumped.

I was over the moon.

On top of that, she still loved me. She didn't say those words, but she didn't have to. I could feel it when I touched her. I could feel it when we kissed. She didn't have to say she loved me. She never said she didn't.

As much as I wanted to be with her, I knew that rushing things wouldn't do me any good. I'd have to be patient and bide my time. I understood that she still needed space. I realized that she needed time to process everything in her head. All I knew was that in the end, she was going to be mine once more.

Alexa and I communicated here and there during the weeks that followed. It wasn't like it used to be, but it was something. I would text her here and there asking about her day, and she'd reply with a couple of sentences. We weren't where I wanted us to be, but at least it was something.

I knew that she needed time, and I was doing the best I could to make sure I was giving her all the space she needed. It required patience on my part, and I've never been known for my patience.

Being without her was driving me crazy. I needed her in my life, and I was really starting to grow frustrated. I wasn't frustrated with her. None of this was her fault. I was frustrated with the situation in general.

After a while, she finally agreed to meet with me. We both decided that there was going to be no expectations when it came to seeing one another. We were just going to talk and see what happened from there. I was all right with that. At the very least, she was open to giving me a chance.

She got off work at 4:00 pm so we made plans to meet at 5:00. I showed up at her apartment right on time, but she wasn't there. I waited for a while before calling her cell phone. She didn't answer. I waited longer and called again with the same result. It was a little after 8:00 when she finally got home.

"Hello, gorgeous. Did you forget we were getting together this evening?" I asked, giving her a quick kiss on the cheek as she approached.

"Nick, this really isn't a good night for me. I think you should just go home, and I'll call you tomorrow."

There was so much hurt and sadness in her eyes. She looked different than I'd ever seen her bore and wondered what was going on.

"Alexa? Are you okay?" I asked as I placed my hand on her shoulder and bent down to be more level with her.

"I've just had a horrible day, and I want it to be over with. Can we please do this another night?"

She looked up at me before unlocking her door. It was hard to get a good look at her in the dark, but once she flipped on her living room light, I could see that she'd been crying.

"Well hold on. Something obviously happened. Is it something I can help with?"

"No, there's nothing you can help with. I promise you that we'll do this another time. I just can't do this tonight. Please just go home, and I'll give you a call tomorrow."

She was begging me to leave, and I thought about turning to go back to my truck, but that didn't feel like the right thing to do.

We might not have been together officially, but I felt like it was still my job to be there for me when she needed me. I couldn't leave her sitting there upset and alone.

"Alexa, you need to let me in. I can see something is bothering you. Let me help you. Just tell me what it is."

She looked up at me, and I could see many layers of pain within her eyes. I'd never seen a person look so sad, and I wanted to know what was causing her such anguish. Eventually, she walked into her living room, sat down on her couch and put her face in her hands.

I closed the door behind me and took a seat next to her on the sofa. I knew she was having a hard time with something, and I didn't want to push her. I would wait until she was ready to talk.

Instead, I placed my hand on her back and rubbed up and down, letting her know I was there for her. I had no idea what could have been on her mind or what I needed to do to help.

"It's my granny," she said after a couple of minutes. "She passed away this afternoon."

When it came to family, Alexa didn't have much of a relationship with any of hers. For the most part, she only had a distant relationship. She had no connection with other family members.

The one exception was her grandmother, who'd she been very close to since she was a little baby. She referred to her grandma as granny.

As her granny got older, most of the family members wrote her off as nothing but an old lady who was more of a nuisance than anything else.

Alexa never saw her that way.

I tried to understand the pain she was feeling, but it was hard for me to do. I didn't have any family to feel connected to and, judging by the pain in her eyes, I was glad I didn't.

At the same time, I knew how she felt about her grandma. She was a really cool person. Alexa had taken me to visit her on a couple of occasions, and we had a blast. She was funny, and the stories she had about Alexa when she was little were priceless.

I hugged Alexa tightly, trying to make her feel secure, and she squeezed me back even tighter. I knew that this was what she needed.

She's a strong, independent woman, but sometimes

you just need another person there to let you know that you're not alone in the world. I kept my arms around as she bawled into my chest. I played with her hair and whispered that things were going to be okay. She was going to be okay, and her grandmother was at peace.

I was saying whatever I could to try to help, but I was confident my words were having little, if any, effect.

"So what happened?" I asked once she had finally calmed down. "How did you find out?"

"I got a call from my mom while I was at work today. Apparently Granny has been in the hospital for a couple weeks, and nobody bothered to call and tell me. She probably thought I didn't care enough to be there with her," she told me, her voice filled with anger and hurt at the same time.

We spent the next few hours talking about her granny. Alexa shared her favorite stories about her and what she was going to miss the most about her.

Late into the night, she fell asleep in my arms. I didn't want to leave her on the couch, so I carried her into bed. Her eyes were so puffy, and her mouth was hanging open so she could breathe.

I tucked her into bed and went into the kitchen, where I left a note on her table. I didn't want her to think that I'd just left as soon as she fell asleep, but at the same time, I wanted to give her the privacy that I knew she needed while still letting her know that I was still there for her.

Alexa,
I just want you to know that I'm here for you. If you need anything at all, please call me.
Nick

22

ALEXA

I had no idea how long I'd been asleep, but the sun was already shining through my window when I opened my eyes.

At first, I freaked out, worrying about what time it was and hoping I wouldn't be late for work. Soon enough, reality smacked me back to earth when I realized that I didn't have to go to work. My granny was gone, and my boss had given me the day off.

The night before was very much a blur. I knew Nick had been at my house, and I'd told him all about my granny. I didn't tell him everything, though.

I didn't tell him that my granny had passed away several days earlier, and my own mother didn't bother to tell me until after the funeral had already taken place. I never even had the chance to pay my last respects or even say goodbye.

I was furious that nobody had the decency to call me and let me know she was sick so that I could visit with her before it was too late. The fact that nobody called me when she died was a slap in the face to me.

In all reality, I shouldn't have been surprised that my family would act like that. It's like they get a kick out of hurting me or something.

Putting those feelings aside, I couldn't help but wonder how I'd gotten into bed. I didn't remember getting sleepy, much less walking myself into my bedroom. I looked around, seeing if maybe Nick was still there somewhere, but I didn't see him, and I didn't hear him moving about anywhere else in the apartment.

I hadn't been able to eat at all after hearing about my granny, and my stomach was rumbling. I still didn't have much of an appetite but figured I better eat something. I wobbled into the kitchen, rubbing my eyes, which were still puffy from so much crying. On the kitchen table was a note from Nick.

While I was cooking my scrambled eggs, I couldn't get Nick off my mind. I thought about how he had insisted on coming into my apartment when I just wanted to be alone.

I wanted to be angry at him for continually being so

bull-headed, but I knew that was just the type of person he was. Besides, having him over had ended up being a good thing.

It was nice to have someone to cry to over losing my granny. It was also nice having someone to vent to about my mother.

Having Nick there allowed me to cry and have someone there to hold me, telling me everything was going to be okay. Having him there also let me get my anger out, which is something I have a problem with. I usually let it fester inside of me until it eventually builds up so much that I feel like I'm going to break.

None of these things did much to ease the pain that came along with losing my granny without getting to say goodbye, but it was nice to know that someone was there for me.

I appreciated the fact that he had been such a gentleman to me. I was in such a vulnerable place that he may have found it easy to take advantage of me. Instead, he tucked me into bed and left me a note letting me know he was there if I needed him.

I wanted to let him know how much I appreciated the gesture, but I didn't want to tell him over the phone. I would go over there later that day and thank him in person.

23
NICK

I was sitting on my bed, looking at the pictures of Alexa that I had hung on my bedroom wall. Anytime I started to miss her, I looked at her pictures and reminded myself that I needed to be patient and hope that she would recognize how much I loved her.

I was deciding whether or not I should go over to her apartment to check on her when I heard someone knocking on my door. I jumped a bit, not expecting to have any company. I thought about ignoring it, hoping whoever it was would go away.

In the neighborhood I live in, it's not uncommon for random people to knock on your door for one reason or another. After another knock, I decided to answer it.

When I opened the door, I was at a loss for words. Alexa was standing on the other side. She looked beautiful. Once the surprise of seeing her there faded, I went into panic mode. Surely she would want to come inside.

How was I going to explain the pictures of her that I'd hung up?

"Hi," Alexa said shyly, not looking like she was all that sure about being there. "Sorry for just dropping by like this. I probably should have called first."

"That's ridiculous. You're fine. How are you?"

"I'm okay, I guess. May I come in?"

I looked back into my apartment, freaking out inside.

"Of course. Come on in," I told her.

I smiled and opened the door so she could come in. I was so nervous. My stomach was in knots, and I was scared of how she was going to react to seeing her pictures.

I knew it probably wasn't going to go well even though I only put them up to look at when I felt lonely. What in the hell was I thinking having them up in the first place?

Alexa came in and started looking around. I'm not really sure what she was looking for. I don't know that she was either. Finally, her gaze fell on my bedroom doorway. She had her back to me, so I had no way to see her reaction, but she sauntered towards the wall, standing in front of it for a minute or two.

Eventually, she turned back towards me. She didn't

look mad or upset at all. The photos didn't seem to have any effect on her at all.

"Yeah, about those. I can explain that," I began to tell her before she held up a hand to stop me.

"Nick, don't even worry about it. I know you're not some crazy psycho guy. You're the most passionate man I know. You just show it in some pretty unconventional ways. I can't hold any of that against you. It's just who you are. Anyway, I wanted to come by and thank you for being there for me last night."

"Thank me for what? You don't have anything to thank me for. I'm just doing what I'm supposed to be doing. I don't care what our official status is, I will always be there for you no matter what."

The sleep that she had gotten the night before had done her a world of good. She looked rested and didn't seem as though she'd been crying nearly as much.

"So what's going on with you tonight?" Alexa asked after a couple of minutes of looking at each other, neither of us exactly sure what to say.

"Honestly? I planned to swing by your place later to check on you, you know, to make sure you were okay after everything you were going through."

I was still having a hard time believing that she was there. It had been so long so since she'd been inside my apartment and all of a sudden, there she was.

"So how are you doing?" I asked. "You doing better today?"

Maybe it was a dumb question to ask, but I sincerely wanted to know how she was. Unfortunately, it caused her entire demeanor to change.

I saw a wave of sadness take over her as she lowered her head to look down at the floor. I thought maybe she was about to start crying. Instead, she breathed in slowly and exhaled just as slow.

"Yeah, I guess I'm doing okay. I'm not good by any means, but I suppose I'm doing better than yesterday," she told me.

I was worried about her and knew she was doing everything she could to keep her hurt and sadness to herself. I knew that she didn't like to drink but thought maybe a drink could do her good under the circumstances.

"Listen, I've got some Old Crow if you're interested in drinking those bad feelings away. It won't get rid of your pain forever, but it'll do the job for the night."

"Old Crow? What is that?" she asked as I made my way to the cabinet, pulling the bottle out. Of course, the bottle was half-gone already. I'd already used it to try to quell the pain of losing her.

"It's what they call bottom shelf whiskey. Just as strong as Jack but a whole hell of a lot cheaper," I told her.

"Whiskey? You know I don't drink that stuff," she

said. After a few moments of contemplation, she decided to go for it. "What the hell, why not? Pour me a glass."

"How about we start with a shot," I laughed.

"A glass, a shot, however in the hell you drink this stuff."

I started laughing at her which, in turn, made her start laughing as well. She was so naive about things like that, and I always found that to be so cute. I grabbed two shot glasses off the counter and filled them with the whiskey.

Alexa sat down at my kitchen table, and I sat across from her, placing her shot on the table. She grabbed it and thought about drinking it but wasn't really sure how to do it.

She watched as I picked mine up and quickly shot it, swallowing it in a single gulp. I tried not to make any reaction even though it burned going down.

She grabbed her shot glass and looked at it like she was already regretting telling me to pour her one. Putting it up to her mouth, she closed her eyes and quickly threw it down the hatch. The look on her face was priceless. She scrunched up her entire face and shook her head back and forth, her tongue sticking out.

"Ugh, that may be the grossest thing I've ever tasted," she said as I sat there trying not to laugh. "Pour me another."

I have to admit, hearing her tell me to pour her

another shot surprised the hell out of me. I poured each of us another shot, and we downed them at the same time.

For the half-hour that followed, the two of us sat around talking and laughing. She added in funny faces and hilarious noises each time she took a shot. The shots had no effect on me whatsoever.

I'd been building up one hell of a tolerance since Alexa and I split up. She was long gone, however. It had only taken four shots, but it was clear that she had already found her limit.

Eventually, she got up and started wandering all around my apartment. I had no idea what she was looking for, and I had a pretty good idea that she had no clue either.

As she made her way into my bedroom, I got up from the table and took a seat on the edge of my bed. She was being hilarious, and I wanted a front-row seat to see what she was going to do next.

She made her way over to my closet and opened the door, where she found some of the things she'd left at my place.

"Oh my God, I've been looking all over for these," she said in a very broken sentence, slurring her words as she spoke.

She spun around in my direction, looking as though she was about to fall down. In her hand, she had the sweater and scarf that she'd left at my house. She looked down at me sitting on the bed, giving me a look that was jokingly angry.

"So why do you have this, boy?" she asked. "Why did you keep these things?"

"You left them here, and they were all I had left of you. I wasn't going to get rid of them."

"What do you mean they were all you had left of me? All these pictures on your wall weren't good enough for ya?" She asked as she tossed the scarf around my neck. She was being playful and giving me a hard time. "I thought this whiskey was supposed to be making me feel better," she said after a big sigh. "I don't believe that it's working. It's not making me feel better."

"The whiskey is just to numb the pain," I told her. "It'll take you some time before you actually feel better but I promise you that it's all going to be okay."

It had been so long since I'd had her and I was yearning for her. I had to have her. I rested one of my hands on her back and ran it up to her shoulders.

"Maybe I can do something to make you feel a little better," I said as she leaned closer to me, moaning lightly as I rubbed her shoulders. "Do you want me to make you feel better?" I asked.

"I do," she replied as I guided her down onto the bed.

I was happy to finally be getting the chance to be with

her again. It had been so long since I'd embraced her and felt the softness of her touch.

"I'm going to take care of you tonight," I told you. "Just lie back on the bed and relax. I want to make you feel good," I whispered into her ear.

Alexa didn't say anything. She just nodded her head and smiled. I gave her a long, deep kiss on the lips before running my lips and tongue down to her neck.

I kissed up and down her collarbone, unbuttoning her jeans as I moved along. I continued kissing her hips as I yanked her pants off her body. My lips kissed over her panties, causing my dick to harden.

Once I had her jeans completely pulled off of her, I tossed them to the side, watching them float to the floor before I crawled on top of her. Alexa looked beautiful lying there on the mattress. She was looking up at me.

She didn't say it, but I could tell that she needed me just as much as I needed her. If she could have some kind of release, she might feel just a little bit better. I wanted to make her feel better, even if it only lasted for a little while.

I moved my hand up her thigh as Alexa slowly spread her legs apart for my touch. I laid down next to her and kissed her neck and shoulders while my fingers traced over her panties. The skin below was so soft and inviting. I couldn't wait any longer.

I moved the thin fabric aside, exposing her

completely. I could feel the heat coming from her body. I took one of my fingers and pushed it inside of her. She was wet and ready for my touch. Using her juices, I wet my fingers and began to slowly rub her clit. She moaned, grabbing my arm.

Before long, Alexa started to squirm and move around under my touch. It hadn't taken her very long, and she was already about to get off. It had been so long since we'd been intimate with each other. It felt like ages since I'd been able to touch her and I'd missed it.

"There you go, go ahead and let go. Go ahead and cum for me," I whispered into her ear as I slid two fingers inside of her and continued rubbing her clit.

Within seconds she was yelling out, her entire body shaking with pleasure. She arched her back, bringing her ass completely off the mattress as her orgasm overtook her.

Once she was done, I slid my fingers out of her, causing her to moan a little more. She looked more beautiful than she'd ever looked before. I was hard as could be but I wanted that night to be all about her, so I played with her hair. She looked like she had indeed taken an edge off. She looked so relaxed.

"Why don't you go ahead and go to sleep. Forget about everything else until tomorrow,"

Alexa didn't put up any resistance. She rolled over onto her side, nuzzling her head in my chest while I pulled up a blanket and held her in my arms while she went to sleep.

I felt like everything was finally right. It had taken a long time to get to that point, but everything was finally right again.

24

ALEXA

I had no clue what time it was. All I knew was that it was sometime at night because it was pitch black outside. I sat up on the bed, and my head instantly started to spin.

Having never been drunk before, I'd never experienced a hangover. If that was what you had to look forward to when you drank, I wasn't sure why anyone touched a sip of alcohol in the first place.

It took me a minute to get my bearings, but I was able to look around and realize that I was still in Nick's apartment. My head was pounding so I laid back down on the pillow and wondered what I had been thinking. I kept trying to talk myself out of going over there.

I kept telling myself that nothing good could possibly come from going to his place. I didn't let those little voices in my head win, however, because I felt like I owed it to him to thank him for being there for me when I needed him the most.

Showing my gratitude was never supposed to end with me in his bed, but there I was. My inhibitions were gone as soon as the whiskey went down my throat and I allowed passion and desire to take over.

Nick was sleeping peacefully next to me, his arm around my waist, just like we always slept. I slid my body to the side, grabbing his hand and moving it away from me.

He moved around and said something indecipherable in his sleep, pulling his arm close to himself as he readjusted his body. It was dark, but I was able to see him using the dim light coming from the bathroom. I couldn't help but look at his face. He was so handsome.

I thought about how well I knew him but at the same time, didn't really know him at all. When it came to the physical aspects of our relationship, I knew him well. I knew every single detail of his body.

I knew what turned him on, as well as the things he didn't like. I knew what made him laugh, and I knew what made him upset. What worried me, however, were the things that I had no clue about.

When it came to his past, I had no idea what was true and what was made up. I had no clue who he was when he was younger or anything about his life before I met him.

All I knew was that he had been to prison after a bar fight got out of hand. I didn't know what prison had been like or what kind of an effect it had on him.

Lying there looking at him was so strange. He seemed so peaceful. Everything seemed so calm. It made me wonder how things progressed the way they did. How did we end up in such a bad spot?

I never would have put up with any of that from any other man, but with him, it was so different. Could it be because I had never been in love with any man like I loved Nick? Could it be because I had never felt the kind of love that he had given to me? Was it really love, though? Was it real?

It sure felt real. When we were together, he'd been so good to me. He was sweet and loving. Honestly, when the truth came out about him being in prison, he was pissed off, but he wasn't mad at me. He never told me that I should mind my own business or anything like that.

He was persistent when it came to getting me back. He let me know that he was there and that he still loved me. He never yelled at me or hit me when I denied his advances. Instead, he just kept making sure I knew he was around.

A few people that I told about it said that I should

have been scared of him. They told me that I should have been concerned at his persistence, but I wasn't worried in any way. I wasn't in fear at any time. I knew that he wouldn't ever hurt me.

Of course, maybe I was just being stupid. I could have made him stop coming around if I really wanted to. The truth was, somewhere deep down inside of me, I didn't want him to stop.

As I pondered all of these feelings, I looked down and watched him sleeping. It always amazed me how such a big, tough guy could look so angelic when he slept. All of his features when softened while he was out.

The lines that I usually saw on his forehead weren't visible. I took my finger and traced it lightly from his cheek down to his chest. His muscles were thick and hard, even as he slept.

"Hey gorgeous," Nick mumbled out of his sleep, his voice sounding throaty and scratchy. "How are you feeling?" he asked me, placing his hand on my arm.

I don't know if it was the alcohol that was still in my system or something else, but it felt like the walls were going to close in on me. I scooted away from him as fast as I could and jumped out of bed. As soon as my feet hit the floor, I regretted my decision. My head was pounding, and I felt dizzy.

"Alexa? Is everything okay?"

"Yeah, I'm okay. I've just got a little bit of a headache. Should have known better than to drink like that. I won't be making that mistake again," I told him as I bent down to put on my jeans. "I think I'm just going to head home."

"What? You're leaving? Why?" Nick asked as he stood up from the bed. "You can't drive home. You've had way too much to drink."

"It's fine. I'm not drunk anymore. I just really have to go. I only meant to stop by for a few minutes. I shouldn't be here.

25

NICK

I was having a hard time trying to process what was happening. I thought that things between Alexa and I were all taken care of. I thought we were good.

For once, she had actually come to me instead of me having to go for her. I didn't make her come to my apartment. She came by herself because she wanted to thank me for being there for her in her time of need. She sat at my table and did shots with me. She allowed me to touch her and be intimate with her.

"Alexa, it may be because I just woke up, but I can't understand what's happening right now," I told her as I rubbed my eyes. "You don't need to go anywhere. Why don't you and I just go back to bed and get some sleep? We can talk about this all when we wake up."

"Nick, I really just need to go. I'm sorry. I didn't mean to lead you on. I just need to think."

"Please, think about what you're doing. Don't you know how much I care about you? Do you have any clue how much love I have for you in this hardened heart of mine? I don't think you have any clue how happy it made me to open my door and see you on the other side. I didn't force you to come here. I didn't make you come here against your will. I'm not going to make you stay here if it's not what you want to do. I just wanted you to know exactly how I feel about you."

Alexa looked down at the floor, not sure how she was supposed to be feeling.

"All I wanted to do was be there for you," I continued. "When you showed up here, the only thing I wanted to do was help you. All I wanted to do was try to make you feel better. I just wanted to do what I could to make you happy. That's all I've ever wanted to do. I just want you to be happy. At this point, I don't care if it's because you're with me or not. I just want you to be happy. You deserve it."

26
ALEXA

Never in my life had I felt so conflicted.

On one hand, I couldn't help but be upset over the secrets he kept from me. At the same time, I was worried about him. I'd never seen him as upset as he was right then.

What made things even worse was the fact that he was having such a hard time dealing with the pain he was feeling. I knew I loved him and, as upset as I was with him, I couldn't imagine my life without him in it.

Seeing him so upset was starting to bother me as well. I walked right up to him and put my arms around his neck.

"I know that you mean everything you just said to me. I can see it in your eyes. I know that you want me to be happy. I'm just drained, and my head is pounding. Please don't be mad at me."

"Mad at you? I could never be mad at you," he whispered into my ear. "I just don't want to lose you. I love you so much. I promise you there'll be no more secrets. I'll be an open book from now on, no matter how painful that might be for me."

"Okay, then why don't we go back to bed and continue this conversation in the morning," I told him, moving him back towards the bed.

I was still so confused.

In fact, I may have been more confused than I was in the first place. The one thing I wasn't confused about was how I felt about the man standing in front of me. Out of everything he had said and done, in the end, all he wanted was for me to stay with him and that's what I was going to do. I was going to start with the night and see how things went from there.

27

NICK

In the bedroom, Alexa and I made love. When I climbed on top of her, I noticed that she didn't spread her legs nearly as far apart as she usually did. It was as though she was reluctant to be with me. After the way I had treated her, it was hard to blame her.

"It's okay, Alexa. I'm not going to hurt you. I promise I'm never going to hurt you again."

I felt her legs open, allowing me to position my body the way I wanted it. Grabbing onto one of her thighs, I slowly guided myself inside of her.

As I felt the tightness of her opening, all of my worries were gone. When I felt how wet she was, I started to realize that everything was going to be okay. She may have been hesitant, but she wanted me just as I had wanted her.

She meant the world to me, and I was going to show her one way or another. I never wanted to let go of her and I'd do anything to protect her for as long as she would allow.

The two of us lying in my bed, making love, made me feel alive again. Like I had a purpose.

Finally, we had another chance. I had another chance.

28

ALEXA

I could feel Nick's body weight pushing me down into the mattress as he slowly moved in and out of me. I felt his girth completely filling me as I felt him deep inside of me.

He felt good. He felt really damn good. After all the things that had happened between us, the lies from months ago, the things earlier that evening, there was no denying how good Nick felt inside me.

As he made love to me, he kept whispering into my ear, telling me how good I felt. He kept telling me he loved me and how much he missed me.

"Tell me you love me, Alexa," he said in my ear. The request caught me off guard. It caught me so off guard, in fact, that I didn't respond to him. "Tell me you love me," he said again, this time thrusting into me a little harder. "Tell me, baby. I want to hear it. Tell me you love me."

I didn't know whether or not I should say it. I loved him a lot, but we still had a lot of things to work on. If I said those three little words and decided to break things off, it would crush him. He grabbed my hands and intertwined my fingers with his, pushing them over my head and down onto the bed. I breathed his name into his ear, hoping that would be good enough for the moment.

"I want you to say it," Nick said as he plunged deeper and harder into me.

I knew what he was thinking. He thought that if he fucked me right, I'd say whatever he wanted to hear. I looked up at him and could see pain and fear in his eyes. "Please tell me you love me," he begged again.

I could feel the tension building up inside of me. I knew I was getting close and was trying my hardest to concentrate on that as opposed to Nick's request.

I closed my eyes and was ready to let my climax unleash when I realized my shoulder was wet. It took me a minute to figure out what was happening. Nick was crying.

He wasn't the type to ever show any kind of emotion, much less cry. It made me feel horrible. I knew that Nick had made many mistakes and bad choices in our relationship. He had lied to me about some pretty important things.

In the end, he owned up to those mistakes and never gave up on what the two of us had together. We'd been apart for months, but he never gave up. I was the only thing he wanted.

What kind of person was I? I could have cut the cord at any time and not given him any attention when he came around.

Instead, I strung him along, allowing him to stay a part of my life but only if he did it from a distance. Why did I do that if I didn't want to be with him? Was I scared to be alone? Did I just want to know that I was desirable? Nick made sure that I knew he appreciated me. Didn't he deserve the same in return? Didn't he deserve love and affection as well? I couldn't hold back any longer.

"I love you, Nick," I yelled out as I grabbed him by the neck and pulled him in close to me. "I love you so much," I told him.

I watched as Nick stopped in mid-motion and looked down at me, shocked that he'd heard the words he wanted so desperately to hear. The truth is, I wasn't just saying them because he wanted to hear them. I said them because I meant them.

"I love you, Nick," I spoke softly.

I told him one more time before bucking my hips up towards him, leading him to grab my legs and pumping in and out of me with a vengeance.

I was moaning loudly as my climax was coming quickly. Nick was pounding me harder and harder until I couldn't take it anymore. I wrapped my legs tightly around him and squeezed as I got off.

Nick began groaning as he came at the same time. He rammed himself into me again as his climax overtook him. He moved in an out a little slower until he finally pulled himself out and collapsed onto the bed next to me, allowing me to curl up in his arms.

He had a smile on his face as we laid there, him playing with my hair and me running my fingers all over his chest. All of his patience had finally paid off. He knew in his heart that we were going to be together again.

Even when it looked like a lost cause, he always had faith. And there I was, I'd told him I loved him for so long. Not only had I admitted my feelings to Nick, but in a way, I'd admitted them to myself as well.

I could see the relief on Nick's face. All of the pain that I'd put him through was washed away. Me being there with him made him happy. It was as though the past had never happened. I understood how he felt.

The pain I'd felt from everything he did didn't seem to

matter anymore. I was there, we were together, and I wasn't going to leave this time. There wasn't anywhere else I'd rather be than right there in his arms.

EPILOGUE

"Are you sure you want to do this?" I asked. "This is your last chance to back out on me if you've changed your mind."

The flashing Vegas lights were bouncing off of her face under the dark night sky as our taxi drove down the strip. Even though we were both tired from the plane ride, our energy was renewed once we were parked in front of the wedding chapel.

"I'd never back out on you!"

She leaned across the backseat of the cab and sweetly kissed me on the cheek.

"You plan on backing out on me?" she asked.

"Are you crazy? I already lost you once and went through hell. I'll never let that happen again. You're mine forever."

We made our way into the Viva Las Vegas wedding chapel where the king of rock and roll was standing in the lobby.

Talk about a jacked up wedding.

But it didn't matter. It wouldn't matter if the Easter Bunny married us. As long as my baby's by my side, that's all that mattered.

"Are you two beautiful people here to tie the knot?" Elvis asked us.

"Yeah," I smiled down at Alexa, wrapping my arm around her as a few go-go girls trotted behind us.

"Well, all right! I can tell you two got a hunka hunka burnin' love inside you." he smiled.

Licking his finger, he flipped the page in a book that was resting on top of his stand and grabbed a pen.

"What's your names?"

"Alexa and Nick," I said.

"All right, you two beautiful people. I'm gonna give you the most beautiful wedding you've ever dreamed of," he scribbled our names in the book. "It'll be about 40 minutes. We have two other couples before you, but feel free to take a look around."

Alexa and I walked away from the desk and headed toward the far end of the chapel where you could purchase various wedding packages and keepsakes.

"Are you sure we should get married here?" she whispered. "What if they're not even able to legally marry us?"

"Nah, it'll be fine. I promise."

She shrugged. "Okay, if you say so."

I watched Alexa examine all the different wedding veils until she found one that she liked. "Do you mind if I get this? I think it'd look cute on me."

"Go ahead, baby. Get whatever you want."

I'd been working extra jobs to pay for this trip so we could take a mini-vacation—just a 3-day, long weekend because of a national holiday—to get married and I'd saved up quite a few bones to pay for everything.

But there was one thing that Alexa wasn't counting on, and that was the ring that I bought her without her knowing.

The two of us had picked out simple gold wedding bands for our wedding night, and that's what we were supposed to get married in, but I didn't feel that was good enough for her. While she was hanging out with Kim, us guys went shopping for a better ring. I spent almost every extra penny that I had worked for and saved up, but she deserved it.

"Nick and Alexa," Elvis yelled out into the lobby. "You're up!"

Alexa and I looked at each other, smiling as we

walked back into the wedding chapel and waited for the priest to step in and marry us.

We were surprised when Elvis started walking down the aisle singing "I Can't Help Falling in Love with You."

"Do you have your own vows or would you like to do a traditional ceremony?" he asked as he reached the podium.

Neither of us had written any vows, and both answered, "Traditional," simultaneously.

As we repeated after him, we finally got to the part where we could say our, "I do's."

"Do you have the rings?" he asked.

We both nodded and produced the rings.

"Repeat after me," he said.

My vows went first, and I could hardly wait for her to see the ring I'd bought her.

"With this ring, I marry you and bind my life to yours. It is a symbol of my eternal love, my everlasting friendship, and the promise of all my tomorrows," I finally repeated after him.

"You may place the ring on the bride's finger," he instructed me.

I pulled the ring out of the box, shielding it with my hand until I slipped it onto her finger.

She noticed it right away.

"Nick!? Oh my God! What is this? This isn't the ring we bought?"

"I know. I wanted to get you something special. Do you like it?"

"Oh my God! I love it!"

After she said her vows and we exchanged rings, we kissed each other, finalizing our ceremony.

"What do you want to do now?" she asked as we stood out on the sidewalk.

"Hookers and blow, baby."

She smacked me in the chest. "You're not funny, Nick!"

"Whatever you want to do, baby. It's all up to you."

She eyed me down before saying, "How about we go to a strip club? Maybe I can pick up some fresh moves to try out on you back at our hotel room?"

"Let's go."

Walking into the club, we sat down near the barkeep and ordered a couple of drinks while we waited for the next performance to begin.

"This is going to be so much fun! I've never been to one of these before," she slammed her glass on the counter, motioning the barkeep to bring her another.

"It's all about the experience," I tipped my glass to her and polished off the rest of my drink. "Can I get a beer?"

"Sure thing," the bartender said.

Waiting for the bartender to bring my beer, I feel a tap on my shoulder.

"What are you doing all the way in Vegas? Did you come all these miles to see me?"

Unsure as to who it was, I turned around and about fell off the barstool when I saw her face.

It was the stripper from back home.

Shit.

Alexa noticed her standing behind me and turned around to see who was talking to me.

"Hi, I'm Alexa," my wife introduced herself.

DEREK'S DARK DESIRES

Subscribe to my Dark Desires newsletter and get a FREE copy of Riot instantly! Riot is a full-length novel that is only available to subscribers!

Once you have your free book, you will have the advantage of knowing when I will be releasing my next title, when I'm having special deals, and you'll be the first to know the next time I have some cool stuff to give away (you can unsubscribe at any time).

newsletter.derekmasters.com

ABOUT THE AUTHOR

Derek Masters is an erotic romance author from the Kansas City, MO area. He graduated from the University of Kansas with a degree in criminal justice, but discovered that writing was his true passion. You can often find him talking sports at local hole in the wall bars or working on his next novel in a crowded coffee shop.

www.derekmasters.com
derek@derekmasters.com
Facebook: derekmasterswrites
Private Facebook Group:
www.facebook.com/groups/dereksdirtysubs
Twitter: @thederekmasters

ALSO BY DEREK MASTERS

Please check out my website for a complete list of all of my novels. If you enjoyed the book you just read, please consider taking a moment to let me know by leaving a review on Amazon and/or Goodreads. I appreciate your support more than I could ever express!

Printed in Great Britain
by Amazon